FOOLISH Regrets

USA TODAY BESTSELLING AUTHOR
JEANA E. MANN

SEAFORTH BILLIONAIRES SERIES

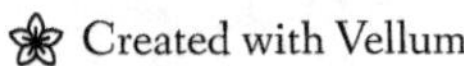 Created with Vellum

FALLON

At the front desk of the Maynard Building, the security guard handed me a temporary access badge with my name printed on it. I pulled the lanyard over my head, then moved to the elevators. As I boarded the car along with a dozen other people, my gaze strayed to the guy beside me. Tall and athletic, he stood with his hands shoved into the pockets of his jeans. Where had I seen him before? He stared straight ahead while I tried not to eyeball him. A gray hoodie stretched over his broad shoulders and hugged a narrow waist. With the hood pulled low over his eyes, I couldn't see most of his features, but I saw his chin. It was square, dimpled, and clean shaven. Desire prickled along my skin. I pushed it aside, turning my focus to the impending interview upstairs.

Focus, Fallon. I ran through a mental list of common interview questions, rehearsing the answers in my head. I needed this job. My brother's future depended on it. The elevator stopped at the tenth floor. A handful of people exited. I cast a sideways peek at Hoodie Guy. Sexual energy rolled off him in waves. I resisted the urge to fan my face and blamed the sudden internal heat on the number of bodies in the elevator. With my load of responsibilities, sex wasn't on the radar, but this guy made my insides do crazy things.

At the next floor, six people boarded. The occupants shifted to make room. My shoulder rubbed against the mystery man. Tingles traveled up my arm. Sensing my gaze, he faced me, lips twitching in amusement. Mortification rushed up my neck and took residence in my cheeks. *Crap!* He'd caught me checking him out. I blushed then looked at the tips of my tennis shoes, the ones I wore for the walk to and from the train, and saw that he was wearing black-and-white Chuck Taylors beneath his faded blue jeans. Odd clothing for a high-profile, professional building.

At the twentieth floor, the elevator emptied, leaving me alone with the hoodie guy.

"Where are you going?" I asked, suddenly aware that he hadn't pushed a destination button, and I was curious to learn where he was going.

"Thirty-five, please." His low, smooth voice instigated a pleasant shiver down my back.

In my head, I heard his voice whispering hot, dirty words in my ear during sex. *No. Oh my God, stop it, Fallon.* Lusting after this guy—any guy—was a pointless endeavor. I bit my lower lip and stared at the door.

"You're going there, too?" he asked.

"Yes. Twisted Wire Productions." The air thickened inside the elevator. My chest felt heavy. Had the air conditioning quit? I plucked at the collar of my blouse. "I've got an interview."

"Is that so?" He lowered his hood. Amazing eyes lined by thick dark lashes drifted to the name badge hanging around my neck. "Fallon Youngblood?"

I liked the way he said my name, slow and easy, with an obvious southern drawl. I liked the way he looked, too. Bohemian. Unique. Dark blond hair curled loosely above his collar, the kind a girl could dig her fingers into. Did I mention he smelled amazing? I wanted to close my eyes and drink in his scent—shower gel, soap, and a hint of peppermint. He took a step closer. A nervous thrill skittered up my arm as our sleeves touched.

"Have we met before?" He cocked his head to the side, processing every detail of my face. My gaze drifted to the leather thong knotted around his neck, the sexy definition of his collarbones, the golden brown of his tan. Definitely not a corporate guy. More like a courier or something.

"No. I don't think so," My voice was breathy, like I'd been running a footrace. The straight slope of his nose and the angle of his square jaw created an unforgettable face. If we'd met, I would have remembered.

"Are you sure? Maybe a club?" He tilted his head to one side. The shift of his body, the way his eyes clung to mine, gave me a pleasant tumble of butterflies in my tummy. I bet he'd broken more than one heart with those eyes, that voice. His lips twitched again, but he didn't smile. I got the feeling smiles were few and far between for this man. "No. You don't look like a club girl." He snapped his fingers. "I know. The train. You took the train this morning?"

"Yes." He'd noticed me. *Me.* Plain Jane, no-frills Fallon Youngblood. A flush of embarrassment burned up my neck to think of him watching while I rooted through my over-sized handbag or stared into space. I'd never caught a man's eye before. Ever. And never one so utterly hot.

"Are you here for an interview?" I asked. Anxiety squeezed my chest. What if I wasn't the right type? What if they wanted someone edgy like him? My hopes for the future were pinned on the possibility of a new and better job.

He shook his head and a flicker of amusement brightened his stormy eyes. "I already work here."

"They let you dress like that?" I heard the judgment in my voice and cringed. I knew what it was like to be judged by my appearance, having existed on the wrong side of fashion since high school. Even if I wanted to wear fancy clothes, my budget didn't allow it. I preferred simple, functional, and sensible.

He glanced down at the concert T-shirt beneath his hoodie. The thin cotton stretched over his torso, showing ripples of abs and pecs. A peculiar energy began to fill the elevator, pulsating and vibrant. My body thrummed in response. With two fingers, he plucked the shirt away from his chest. "You don't like Def Leppard?"

"No. I do. They're fine. It's just—where I work, we have a very strict dress code. No jeans, no tennis shoes, no sleeveless shirts."

"I don't think a person's work should be judged by their appearance, do you?" His gaze roamed over my nice, but secondhand, suit.

"No, I don't. But most of the world does," I said. An unfortunate truth, in my experience. I shopped online for classic, affordable clothes to wear to work. When I was off the clock, I preferred yoga pants and tees. "First appearances are everything. Most people make up their mind about you within the first twenty seconds."

"Most of the world has it wrong."

The conversation reminded me it was time to change shoes. Dress for success, my mother had always said, and I took her words to heart. I dug a pair of high-heeled pumps out of my bag. I rested a hand against the elevator wall for balance, removed my tennis shoes, and slipped on the high-heeled pumps, conscious of the guy's eyes upon me. Aside from the aura of intrigue around him, he seemed like a regular person. Scuffs marred his Converse. His jeans were faded almost white, the hems frayed, and a tiny rip at the knee. They hung on his narrow hips like an old friend.

He cocked his head to one side. "I've met some brilliant people, and their clothes had nothing to do with their success."

"Really?" I arched a skeptical eyebrow.

"Yeah. Really." His chuckle brought another blush to my cheeks.

The car stopped on our floor, and I felt disappointed. A million questions bubbled to my lips. I wanted to know more about him. Where did he get the scar on his forehead? Where was he from? His intelligent eyes intrigued me. I had a feeling there was a story hidden somewhere in their depths, a story worth hearing. One I'd never learn once we left the elevator.

The doors opened. Remembering my upcoming interview, my hands began to tremble. I had a lot at stake. As the sole support for my invalid brother Hank, the list of my financial responsibilities was long and growing longer by the day. With my current job, I barely kept my head above water.

"Nice to meet you," the guy said and gestured for me to exit. Before I could ask his name, he disappeared into a hallway at the left of the reception area.

A curious sense of loss faded into numbness. Most twenty-three year olds would have flirted with a hot guy like him. Not me. I shut down the fun-loving girl inside and shoved her into the dark recesses of my soul. That part of my life was over, possibly forever. No more dating or fun.

The idea of a future with a member of the opposite sex seemed ludicrous given my circumstances. I straightened the collar of my blouse and drew in a deep breath. Dreaming about the future was a waste of brain power. As a rule, I focused on the present, and never, ever dwelled on the past.

2

TUCKER

Once I left Fallon in the lobby, I went to my desk and sank into the chair. I looked forward to seeing her board the train every morning. With six new cars in the garage and a ten-digit bank account, I didn't need to ride the train anymore, but downtown traffic was a bitch, and I liked the normalcy. Little things like that kept me grounded in a world where everyone wanted a piece of me or my fortune. I always sat in the back row of the train car, next to the window, hoodie pulled over my head, to shield me from view. Most of the time, I remained unnoticed, but every now and then, some kid would recognize me and ask for an autograph. Fame had never been my goal in life. That had always been Sydney's thing. The thought of my ex-girlfriend sent an arrow of angst straight to my heart.

Fallon seemed like the epitome of normal. I'd never intended to talk to her, but sharing the confined elevator space had broken my silence. Over the past few months, I'd contented myself with watching her on the train, imagining the details of her life, wondering what made her doe eyes so sad. She never spoke to anyone, never looked around, never smiled. She just sat in her seat, forehead leaning against the window, and stared at the passing scenery. Did she have a husband who neglected her? Had she lost someone she loved? My fertile imagination ran wild thinking up possible scenarios.

An aura of heartbreak surrounded her, drew me to her. We had that in common—the heartbreak. I wanted to comfort her, tell her I understood how it felt to be sad, but I didn't know how to approach her without sounding creepy or weird. On the flip side, I didn't want to become invested in someone else, like I'd become invested in Sydney. Sydney with the raven hair, the ruby-red lips, and the mischievous eyes. She'd stolen my heart then stomped on it like I'd meant nothing to her, while she'd been everything to me.

Anger replaced my pain. No woman would ever play me like that again. I stood up from the desk and paced around the room. The place was in shambles due to the ongoing remodel, and I stumbled over a stray box of ceiling tiles. I kicked it at the exact moment Caleb came into the room.

"Knock much?" I asked, directing my anger at him, since he was convenient.

"Don't be a dick." He flopped onto the sofa sitting haphazardly in the center of the office. He brushed his sandy hair out of his eyes, unaffected by my mood, and watched me pace. "What's eating you? You're going to wear out your shoes."

"Nothing." His words snapped me back to reality. I returned to my chair and propped my feet up on the desk. He was my brother Tate's best friend, and my business partner. He knew my moods but didn't seem concerned by the black cloud hanging over my head on this particular day.

"Someone's pissy." A smirk tilted the corners of his lips. "You know, a good lay would cure what ails you."

I glared at him. Even my coworkers knew about my epic dry spell. I hadn't been with anyone since Sydney, hadn't even given it a thought. The idea of baring my body and soul to a woman made my heart shrivel—if I still had a heart. I wasn't really sure anymore. "Are you here to discuss my sex life, or do you have business to talk about?" I snapped and immediately regretted it. It wasn't his fault my life was a fucked-up mess. I blamed Sydney for that, for stealing the sunshine from my world. I sat back in the chair, hating the person I'd become, hating Sydney for turning me into a bastard.

"No, actually, I'm here because I had a radical idea last night. I think I know how to pull you out of your funk." He moved from the cushions to perch on the arm of the sofa. He held up an index finger. "Two words. Seaforth Towers."

"What about them?" I asked, deciding to humor his latest epiphany. The muscles across my forehead pulled tight. I knew the place. The twin skyscrapers were the tallest structures in the city and belonged to Maxwell Seaforth, the father of my best friend, Sam. I might be a bastard, but I had nothing on Maxwell. He was a cold-hearted son of a bitch, multi-billionaire, and ruthless human being.

"They're the perfect place for a BASE jump."

I stared at him, my troubles forgotten for a moment. Over the past year, Caleb and I had taken our passion for skydiving to the next level. I'd completed three of the four components by hurling myself off bridges, antennas, and the occasional mountainside, but I had yet to tackle the fourth element—a manmade structure. BASE jumping chased away the numbness, made my blood sing, made me *feel* in a way I hadn't for the past year. It was dangerous and foolish, and I loved every minute of it. Maybe he had something here. For the first time in a long time, I felt excited.

"Sounds like a perfect way to go to jail." Reservations tempered my enthusiasm. "Those buildings are locked up like Fort Knox. Even if we could get to the roof, the cops would be there before we hit the ground. We'd need spotters, a way past security." I shook my head. "It's too complicated."

"I know. I've thought about that." He crinkled his nose, the same way he had in fourth grade when he'd plotted mischief with my brother. "And I've got all the details worked out."

3
____

FALLON

As I waited for the receptionist, my palms began to sweat. After the nerve-wracking elevator ride, I had difficulty bringing my thoughts back to the interview. For the better part of three years, I'd worked for Reyes Media in the accounting department. The modest salary paid for my incidentals and utilities, but not Hank's astronomical medical expenses. Government assistance paid for the majority of his care. I did what I could to help out, but it wasn't nearly enough. Twisted Wire Productions offered better pay and benefits, something I needed desperately.

The receptionist lowered the phone from her ear and gave me the once over through eyes outlined by heavy blue pencil. "You're late." Disapproval lent a sour note to her words. "Lucky for you, they're running a little behind this morning." She wore pink cargo pants, her short hair pulled into a dozen tiny pigtails around her head, tied off with rainbow elastics. "Follow me."

She pushed through the double doors behind her desk without a backward glance. I trotted after her. The doors opened into a vast area of organized chaos. People milled from one desk to another. Rock music played through speakers, drifting below the hum of conversation and laughter. No one seemed older than thirty, and they were all dressed in various degrees of casual attire—blue jeans, football jerseys, and concert T-shirts. It seemed more like a party than a business.

My heels clacked on the tile floor as we circumvented a large sectional sofa and a cluster of workstations. A guy with two hoops piercing his eyebrow jerked his chin in greeting. I tugged at the hem of my blazer, cognizant of the disparity in our appearances. What kind of place was this? Too late, it occurred to me that I should have done more research on the company. I knew little about Twisted Wire Productions except it was new and making a name for itself in video game design.

The receptionist knocked on a closed door then opened it to reveal a conference room. A tumble of nerves flitted in my stomach.

"Fallon? I'm Denise Washington, head of Human Resources. Please come in." A tiny, grandmotherly woman stepped forward to shake my hand. She motioned to a chair beside the conference table. "We'll begin in just a moment. We're waiting on Mr. Spaulding."

Mr. Spaulding? A new wave of panic set in. Tucker Spaulding, president and CEO of Twisted Wire Productions, was coming to my interview? I cleared my throat. "Does Mr. Spaulding always sit in on interviews?"

"When he can," Mrs. Washington said. She motioned toward a table along the far wall. "Would you like something to drink? Coffee, water, soda?"

"No, thank you." A heavy, uncomfortable silence fell over the room. I clasped my hands in my lap, trying not to fidget. The Spartan décor of the room didn't help my anxiety. The walls were a cold gray, the floors neutral slate, and the furnishings minimalist. Framed posters of video games provided the only color in the room.

The doors opened on silent hinges. The guy from the elevator walked into the room, a package of powdered doughnuts in one hand and a Red Bull in the other. Somewhere between the elevator and the conference room, he'd ditched the gray hoodie. His concert T-shirt stretched tight over his chest. "Sorry for the delay," he said.

I tried not to stare. Sexual awareness licked up my thighs. I swallowed down conflicting emotions and glanced at Mrs. Washington for an explanation.

"Good morning, Mr. Spaulding," she said.

My head exploded. Hoodie Guy was the CEO. *Great. Strike one.* After I'd ribbed him for his casual attire, he probably thought I was a total ass. Not to mention the way I'd been checking him out in the elevator. I drew in a deep breath and tried to rein in my lust. A crush on my potential boss spelled trouble with a capital T. Thoughts of Hank and his future needs renewed my determination. I wasn't here for myself. I was here for him.

"Good morning." Mr. Spaulding took a seat at the head of the table. His biceps strained against the sleeves of his shirt as he lifted the Red Bull to his mouth. Thick-lashed eyes met mine, and my girly parts squeezed.

"Mr. Spaulding, this is Fallon Youngblood." Mrs. Washington handed him a file folder with my name on the tab.

"We met in the elevator," he said, still staring at me. I stared back, unable to look away, our gazes locked.

"She was late, sir," Mrs. Washington said.

No, no, no, no. I'd committed the cardinal sin of interview etiquette. *Strike two.* My chances at getting the job shriveled in front of my eyes. I glanced down at the table, mentally calculating the odds of completing this meeting without appearing to be a total loser.

"Yeah. Me, too. It wasn't our fault. The train was delayed. Want one?" The plastic wrap of the doughnut package crinkled as he held the box in front of me.

"Um, no. I'm fine. Thanks."

"Suit yourself." He withdrew one of the round confections and popped it into his mouth then opened the folder and thumbed through my application with sugary fingers. After a few nerve-wracking minutes, he kicked back in his chair, rested his ankle on the opposite knee, and regarded me across the table. "Okay, I'm ready. Go ahead, Mrs. Washington."

The woman ran through a litany of questions. Most of them were standard fare. I answered by rote, grateful I'd rehearsed my answers ahead of time, aware of Mr. Spaulding's unnerving gaze on my face. Beneath the table, I clenched my hands into tight fists. *Breathe, Fallon. Stay calm. You can do this.*

"I don't see your college or university listed here," Mrs. Washington said. The lines in her forehead deepened. *Strike three.* My hopes plummeted.

"I don't have a degree," I replied, and lifted my chin a notch. "But I have more than enough experience. I've worked in the accounting department for three years, and I'm skilled in coding and programming."

"A college degree is a requirement for this position." She shook her head and looked at her employer, one eyebrow raised, posing a delicate question. His head tilted to the side in what seemed to be his signature gesture. A silent conversation passed between them. "I'm not sure how she got through the applicant screening process. I'm sorry."

Tucker studied me for an uncomfortable beat. I stared back, humiliation churning my insides. A college degree in computer programming had always been my dream, but after Hank's accident, I'd given up any hopes of furthering my education. I'd fallen into the accounting gig by accident, starting out as a customer service rep and filling in for vacations in the payables department, working my way up, learning and advancing with each promotion. Now, I'd hit a brick wall at Reyes Media, unable to advance without a degree. Fate continued to knock me into the dirt every time I tried to better myself.

"Thank you for your time. I can see myself out." I lurched to my feet, eager to put an end to this fiasco. The chair tipped backward and nearly overturned with the awkward force of my movements. I scrambled to keep it upright. Tucker's hand snaked out. He grabbed the chair and eased it back onto its legs.

"It's okay." He gestured for me to sit. I lowered into the chair. "Ms. Youngblood, you obviously feel you're qualified for the job or you wouldn't be here." His tone softened. "Convince me."

My mind scrambled to gather a rebuttal. Inside my shoes, my toes tapped a frantic rhythm. I swallowed and found curious eyes regarding me, devoid of judgment or prejudice. Looking into their clear depths soothed my anxiety. I had the skills and the experience. I could do this. "Well." I paused for a deep, cleansing breath before continuing. "I've been overseeing seven hourly associates for the past year. I issue checks each week, balance the ledgers, and run all the weekly financial and job costing reports for the company. I've also designed and implemented programs to streamline our reporting practices. I'm patient, easy to talk to, and I've been voted Employee of the Month seven times." My voice quivered on each word. He nodded in approval. I drew in a deep breath and unclenched my fingers.

Tucker leaned forward, his eyes never leaving mine. "Good. That's great. Have you ever played *Dragons of Destiny*?"

My heart sank. I'd heard of *Dragons of Destiny*. It was the most popular video game franchise in the world and even had a movie in production. Hank had adored the game when it first came out, playing it into the wee hours of the morning, keeping me awake on school nights, but I'd never played it, never even seen it. My lifestyle didn't afford time for frivolity.

"Um, no." My knee bounced beneath the table, sloshing the contents of Mr. Spaulding's Red Bull. I slapped a hand on my thigh to still the movement. "I'm sorry. I haven't. But I'm not really sure what that has to do with this position."

"Nothing. Just curious." A glimmer of mischief flickered in his eyes, then extinguished. Where did it go? I wanted the playful light to come back. Something about it called to me. He reached for another doughnut.

"Mr. Spaulding, I'm sorry to interrupt. I wanted to remind you about your appointment?" The receptionist poked her head into the conference room, a blinding smile on her face for Tucker.

"Right. Thank you. I'm on my way." He nodded, breaking our eye contact to stand. "I'm sorry. I've got to go, but I think we're done here anyway. Mrs. Washington will show you to the elevator."

I stood and offered my hand. "Thank you for your time."

"You're welcome." Warm, strong fingers wrapped around mine as we shook hands. Attraction zinged up my arm. He stiffened and pulled his hand away. Had he felt it too? I pressed my palm against my leg to stop the lingering vibrations.

We all moved to leave at the same time. He opened the door for me. As I passed through the opening, my body hummed at his proximity. I held my breath and stepped outside then exhaled once we had a few feet of distance between us. Mrs. Washington trailed behind and spoke to him in a low voice. "Doughnuts and Red Bull for breakfast? Really, Tucker? All that sugar isn't good for you."

"Geez, give me a break, Grandma." His tone held a note of affection. *Grandma?* I turned in time to catch a glimpse of her brushing the hair away from his forehead. The profile view of their faces revealed the same straight nose and high cheekbones. If the resemblance wasn't enough to confirm their relationship, the woman's obvious tenderness convinced me. I pressed my lips together to repress a smile.

"I'll order out and get something good for you," she said. "You need protein." Her hand lowered to cup his cheek. "You look so tired. Still not sleeping?"

"Grandma, not in front of everyone." He shrugged away from her touch, a ghost of a smile teasing his mouth.

"Oh, sorry. My bad." She patted his arm.

Their exchange tugged at my heart. I missed my grandparents; they'd passed away years ago, but it was good to see someone enjoying his. It reminded me there were still normal families in the world, that maybe there was hope for my shattered family after all.

"Later, gators." He lifted a hand in dismissal. I nodded and watched him disappear through an office door.

Once he exited the hall, Mrs. Washington walked me to the elevator, professional demeanor restored. "We intend to make a decision by the end of the week. You'll hear back from us one way or the other."

The sympathetic smile on her lips told me I had zero chance of getting this job. Crushing disappointment weighted my shoulders. After my parents died, Hank and I had received a tidy but dwindling amount of life insurance money and the deed to our family home. Under normal circumstances, the money would have lasted a lifetime, but Hank's condition required a monumental amount of funds. I wanted to give him the best care, and it wasn't going to happen with my paltry current salary.

"Thank you for your time. I appreciate the opportunity to interview with Mr. Spaulding," I said to break the uncomfortable silence.

"He's a good person to work for," she said. Genuine warmth lit her eyes. "He knows every person in his employment by name. I'm very proud of him. He's done all this on his own."

"That's quite an accomplishment for someone so young. For anyone, really. He's not anything like I expected."

She smiled, and her blue eyes twinkled, revealing pride and love. "No. He's not. He's one of a kind."

After the interview, I went on to my regular job and tried to catch up on my work. I'd told my boss I had a dentist appointment, so no one questioned my late arrival. I plowed my way through stacks of invoices and statements. My workload continued to increase with each passing week, and I'd taken to working from home in the evenings to stay current. At precisely five o'clock, I shut down my computer, packed up my laptop, and headed to the bank of elevators. Hank's nurse, Hillary, got off work at six, and

I needed to be there to take care of him when she left. She didn't mind staying over from time to time, but tonight was her granddaughter's recital. I knew how important it was to her and didn't want her to miss a minute of it.

While I waited for the elevator to arrive, my anxiety climbed along with it. I needed to leave precisely at five in order to catch the five-fifteen train. With the entire building rushing to leave, it took forever for the car to ascend to the top. The minutes crawled past. I eyed the stairs as my next option. Thirty-five floors were a lot to descend, but I couldn't bear to be late. Just when I'd decided to tackle the steps, Andrew Harper, my boss, opened his office door and made a beeline for me. *Crap.*

"Ms. Youngblood, can I see you for a minute?" The sound of his high voice whined in my ear like a mosquito.

"Um, sure. I only have a minute. What do you need?"

"I didn't get the weekly recap today." He peered at me down his long, thin nose and licked his lips. He even looked like a mosquito. "Is there a problem?"

"It's not due until tomorrow afternoon." I tried to hide the irritation in my voice. He was always doing this, deriding me for missing deadlines I didn't know existed, switching up the requirements of my job at the last minute.

"I told you I wanted it today." He glared and gestured with his hands.

"No. You didn't. And I can't run the report anyway until tomorrow. LaTanya gives me the information on Tuesdays." Andrew was the kind of manager who had no idea what his employees did during the day. He existed purely for paper and numbers on reports.

"How am I supposed to do my projections? This oversight is inexcusable." With thumb and forefinger, he pinched the bridge of his nose. "Get LaTanya on the phone and tell her to get the information up to you. Now."

"LaTanya called off today. Her son was sick." Which he should have known.

"Fine. Have it on my desk first thing tomorrow. I don't care what you have to do to get the information, just make sure it's there." He groaned and squeezed his eyes closed. "This lapse is going into your review, by the way."

I opened my mouth to defend myself, then thought better of it. Experience had revealed the futility of arguing with Andrew. "I'm sorry, but I really have to get going." I glanced nervously at my watch. Five-thirteen. No way would I make the first train now. The next one left at five-thirty, putting me a half hour late. Hillary wasn't going to be pleased, not that she'd ever complain, but I hated to take advantage of her.

"I hope this isn't going to become a habit, Ms. Young-blood, coming in late and leaving early. I realize you have challenges at home, but please don't use them as an excuse to abuse the company's generosity. If you come in late, I expect you to stay over to make up the time." With a skinny finger, he pushed his glasses up the bridge of his nose.

"I really have to go." On the outside, I remained calm. Inside, my temper seethed. I bit back the acerbic words on the tip of my tongue. I skipped lunch every day, worked from home every night, and covered for absent employees while keeping up with my own duties. In spite of Hank's numerous hospital visits and frequent illnesses, I never called off. The stupid weekly report wasn't even my responsibility; it was his. Somehow I'd gotten roped into doing a substantial amount of his work, work for which he claimed all the glory and gave me none. In the nick of time, the elevator chimed, and the doors opened. I jumped inside.

"Can we talk about this tomorrow? I promise to have the report on your desk first thing."

He opened his mouth to reply, but the doors slid shut between us. I squeezed my eyes closed and counted to ten. The walls of my life seemed to be closing in around me, strangling me. One of these days, my temper was going to snap and Andrew would fire me. I couldn't afford to lose this job, not until I had something better lined up.

By the time the elevator reached the ground floor, it was five-twenty. I sprinted out the revolving doors and down the crowded sidewalk, fighting the throng of people. I managed to jump on the last train car mere seconds before it departed. Breathing hard, I slid into a window seat near the back. Adrenalin still raced through my veins, anger at Andrew and life in general building with each passing minute. I couldn't seem to catch a break, personally or professionally.

My fingernails cut into the palms of my hands. As the city buildings raced by the speeding train car, I focused on my breath, inhaling, exhaling, slowing the rush of air into my lungs. I might not be able to manipulate fate, but I possessed the power to regulate my reactions to it. When my breathing returned to normal, I relaxed each of my fingers. The tension gradually slid out of my muscles. I didn't want Hank to see me as anything other than calm. He had enough stress in his life without the burden of mine.

Outside the train, skyscrapers and warehouses turned into residential homes. I settled into the seat and tapped out a quick apology text to Hillary. She responded with a smiley face, putting my worries at ease until I felt the weight of someone's stare on the back of my head. I turned to find Tucker two seats away, eyes locked on me.

Hoping he was looking at someone else, I turned toward

the window, bit the inside of my cheek, and studied the flashing scenery outside.

"Hey." His deep, male voice vibrated in my ear, close enough to raise gooseflesh on my neck.

"Hey." I glanced sideways to find he'd moved up to the seat behind me. I ducked my head and studied my phone, pretending to ignore him. The unexpected attention caused me to fidget in my seat.

"Twice in one day. What are the odds?" He leaned his forearms on the seat-back and rested his chin on his wrist, inches from my shoulder.

"It's three times, really. The elevator, the interview, and now," I replied. The smell of his shampoo and body wash wafted through the air between us. I drew in a deep breath and savored his clean, masculine scent. *No, Fallon. What are you doing? You don't go around smelling men.* I leaned away, putting as much space as possible between us, and tried to breathe through my mouth. "I don't usually take this train."

"Me neither." He slid his tongue over his lower lip, drawing my eyes to them by a force beyond my control.

I shifted in the seat to face him. Since I had no chance of getting the job, I felt free to unleash my frustration. "You could've told me who you were in the elevator, *Mr. Spaulding*."

"I didn't want to ruin the surprise. You've got to admit it was a good one." He shoved back in his seat, withdrew a pair of black sunglasses from his pocket, and perched them on his nose, hiding his eyes. "And call me Tuck."

"I don't like surprises," I said. "Especially at job interviews. It was embarrassing." Humiliating seemed a better choice of description. I wanted to put the entire incident behind me, an impossible task with him sitting less than a foot away. Just looking at him reminded me of my failures.

"Would you have believed me if I told you who I was in the elevator?" Even though I could no longer see his eyes, I felt them roam over my face, assessing.

"Probably not."

Long fingers shoved through the mess of his dark blond hair, and he almost—*almost*—smiled. I held my breath in anticipation of the upward curve of his mouth, but it didn't happen. "Let me make it up to you. Wanna get a coffee or something?"

For one crazy moment, I considered it. Every fiber of my being wanted to say yes. I longed to hang out, to act my age, to be carefree, if only for a few hours. The old Fallon would have jumped at a chance to hang with a pretty bad boy. After Hank's accident, I'd been too busy with work and his care to enjoy the company of anyone, let alone a hot young man. The friends I'd had before the accident had drifted away. I understood their need to distance themselves from the awkwardness of the situation. Heck, I wanted distance myself. Most of the time, I tried not to dwell on the consequences of my responsibilities, but caring for Hank was a choice I made willingly. Nothing mattered more than his wellbeing.

"Thanks, but I can't." I faced forward and hoped he'd take the hint. If he asked again, my defenses might crumble, and I might do something reckless like take him up on the offer.

"You don't like coffee?"

I drew in a lungful of air and tried to think of a way to be polite while getting the point across. "I love coffee. But no."

"Why?" He cupped a hand and sniffed his breath, a

gesture that might have made me laugh if I hadn't been so drained from the day. "Do you find me repulsive or something?"

"No, you know you're hot. I just—" I stopped myself. No one understood the monumental responsibilities in my life. I'd given up trying to explain them years ago. There were no adequate words to describe Hank's total dependency on me, our tragic past, and our bleak future. Thank goodness, my stop was in sight. I gathered my belongings and prepared to rush from the train the second it slowed. Tucker's brow furrowed. A wave of guilt made me reconsider the bluntness of my words. I did my best to smile, but my cheeks ached like they might crack from the strain. "Look. It's not you. It's just—well, I don't have time for dating. And the whole deal with the interview makes this a little weird, don't you think?"

4

TUCKER

The invitation to coffee had slipped out of my mouth before I could stop it. Once it was out there, I couldn't take it back, so I zipped my lips and waited for Fallon's answer. When she declined, I breathed an inward sigh of relief. It had been months since Sydney had married someone else, but I wasn't prepared to move on. Not yet. Maybe not ever.

My heart skipped a beat when Fallon's eyes met mine. I told myself the race of my pulse and the dryness in my mouth meant nothing. The wounded depths of her eyes pulled me in. I knew wounded. I saw it every morning when I looked in the mirror, felt it every night when I went to bed.

From behind the safety of my shades, I studied her profile. Her nose was a tad bit long, her cheekbones too high, and her chin pointed, but as a whole, her features worked together to make an arresting face. When she moved, sunlight sparked streaks of red and gold in her light brown hair. She was so different from Sydney. Fallon's hair was coiled in a tight bun at the nape of her neck, every strand controlled and in place. There were no traces of cosmetics on her porcelain skin, her lips naturally pink. Sydney never left the house without full makeup, always prepared for her fans or the paparazzi, a smile painted on her lips. I'd never seen her face bare or her hair mussed. Next to Sydney's contrived appearance, Fallon seemed real, genuine, refreshing.

Fallon stood as the train rolled up to her station. She looked as relieved as I felt to be parting ways. ""It was nice to meet you. Goodbye." She kept her chin tucked to her chest and her eyes down, avoiding my gaze.

"Later," I replied, determined to shrug off her rejection, confused by my disappointment. I watched as she hurried down the platform, shoulders hunched, tension throughout all the lines of her thin body. As she passed beneath my window, a barrel-chested man jostled her. Her wallet fell out of her purse and landed on the platform a few feet from the train. Fallon hurried in the opposite direction, oblivious.

Before the doors closed, I bolted off the car and snatched up her wallet. The train moved down the track with a quiet electronic hum. I broke into a jog along the platform, hoping to reach her before she left the station. I could always catch another train or call Tate to come and get me. When I rounded the corner of the ticket office, Fallon had already vanished down the street.

5

____

FALLON

I trudged up the sidewalk to my house, careful to step around the weeds sprouting through the cracks in the concrete. Loose boards on the porch floor groaned beneath my weight. I made a mental note to call a handyman for the repairs once I'd saved enough money, a day that might never come. The front door squeaked shut as I stepped into the foyer. After the long day, my feet ached, and I had no energy, but I forced a bright tone into my voice and called out to Hank. "Hey, buddy."

He didn't answer. He never answered, because a traumatic head injury had damaged the speech center of his brain. Instead, he stared at me from the hospital bed in our living room. Large amber eyes wrung my heart in a thousand different ways. Seeing him among the white bed linens, motionless, gave perspective to the world. The interview didn't matter. Tucker Spaulding didn't matter. I had no right to feel sorry for myself. I had the use of my body and a life beyond the confines of our house. Hank had nothing. Nothing but me.

"Did you have a good day?" I took a seat on the edge of

his bed and smoothed the covers over his chest. He shook his head. I looked to Hillary, his private duty nurse, for confirmation.

"We had a good day." Hillary lived in the spare bedroom and stayed with Hank while I went to work. Her sturdy form towered over us, kind eyes smiling. While he glared at her, she adjusted the incline of his bed with gentle hands. "Don't you give me the stink eye, mister." She laughed at his dismay and gave me a wink. "It was bath day. He hates that."

"Don't I know." I patted his cheek, one of the few places on his body with sensation.

Hank could be challenging on the best of days. Not that I blamed him. It had to be difficult, to be seventeen and confined to a bed forever. He spent his days and nights within the four walls of the living room. I'd tried to brighten the space with yellow paint and provided stimuli through television and audiobooks. No amount of color or sound, however, could replace the use of his legs or the loss of his future.

Hillary fluffed a pillow then placed it behind his head. "He's got a bed sore on his left hip. Keep an eye on it. Make sure you turn him in an hour." After we'd gone over the rest of his status for the day, she said, "If you don't need anything else, I'm going to get out of here."

"Sure. No problem," I shooed her toward the door. "I'm so sorry I was late. Have a great evening. And tell Les hello for me." The evenings were hers to enjoy on her own. She often spent the time with her boyfriend, Les, who lived a few blocks down the street, or visiting her grandchildren.

"I will." She patted my shoulder. "Call me if you need me."

Once I made sure Hank was settled and comfortable, I

stripped out of my work clothes and donned sweats and a T-shirt. While leftovers heated in the microwave, I grabbed my laptop and set up shop in the living room, where I could keep an eye on him and work at the same time.

I'd just sat on the bed next to him with a bowl of chicken soup when he groaned. "What's wrong?" A fine sheen of perspiration glimmered on his forehead. "Are you in pain?" His quick nod confirmed my suspicions.

Since the accident, I'd grown accustomed to the unglamorous task of caring for my brother's needs. Because he was paralyzed from the chest down, those duties included emptying his catheter and colostomy bags, feeding, and bathing him. After years of practice, the sight of his naked body no longer embarrassed me, but Hank hated for me to touch him that way. The doctors said he comprehended everything we said and did, in spite of his muteness. I knew he understood by the way he gritted his teeth whenever I washed his rear end.

I found his pain medication and the chart, which Hillary kept to track his meds. After verifying the time of his last dosage, I meted out the pills to dull his constant pain. It killed me to see his long body wasting away in a bed. Before the accident, he'd been a handsome and strong teenager, popular, quarterback of the junior high football team, an honor student, and a cross country runner. Now, he spent his hours confined to a fifteen-by-twenty-foot space.

"There. That should help," I said after he'd swallowed the second tablet. He turned his face to the window and stared outside, refusing to acknowledge me. I tried not to take the snub personally, but his rejection still hurt. "It's almost time for the baseball game. Do you need anything else before we eat?"

Usually, the mention of sports perked his spirits, but tonight he continued to stare out the window. By now, the food was cold. I returned to the kitchen and reheated the soup in the microwave. I tested a bite to make sure it wasn't too hot before I settled on the edge of the bed and lifted a spoonful to his mouth. He pressed his lips tightly together and turned his head away.

"Hank, you have to eat." When I insisted, he twisted to and fro. His shoulders retained enough function to knock the bowl from my hands. The liquid soaked the sheets, his pajamas, and the front of my shirt. "Way to go. Now I'm going to have to change the sheets and our clothes." Which meant more laundry. Like I had time for that. I held my temper in check but couldn't prevent a heavy sigh from escaping. When I tried to unbutton his shirt, he squirmed and wiggled until we were both out of breath from the struggle. "What's gotten into you?"

Most of the time, he was sweet and even-tempered, but sometimes, when the reality became too much, he snapped, and I couldn't hold it against him. I pushed his brown hair back from his forehead and tried to read his thoughts through his eyes. Twin red patches colored his cheeks. A tear of frustration rolled down his nose and quivered at the tip. I dabbed at the tear with a tissue then followed his gaze out the window.

Neve Michaelson, our neighbor, sat on her porch, holding hands with a boy. Several minutes later, a car pulled into her driveway. Six teenage kids spilled onto the pavement. Their laughter wafted through the open window. The lightbulb went off inside my head. Once upon a time, those kids had been Hanks friends. Neve had been Hank's girlfriend. Now, she was just a vision through the window, a bitter reminder of the life he no longer lived.

"Oh, Hank, I'm so sorry." I cupped his cheek in my hand. The stubble on his chin scratched my palm. He needed a shave. When had that happened? When had my baby brother changed from a boy to a man? My heart ached for him, for everything he'd lost; the parties, the dates, the laughter. Because I didn't know what else to do, I crawled into the bed beside him, wrapped my arms around his neck, and held him.

6

TUCKER

eeling like a voyeur, I peered into Fallon's wallet. The mysterious depths of a woman's personal items had always frightened me a little. After a tentative search, I found her driver's license. According to the map search on my phone, the address was only a few blocks to the south. I hopped over the curb, cut down an alley, and set out in the direction of her house.

People lingered on their front porches and waved as I entered Fallon's neighborhood. Classic turn-of-the-century houses rested in the center of spacious yards. The curving branches of aged trees formed a leafy canopy over the streets. Children played on the wide sidewalks, and the smell of barbecue lingered in the air. My stomach growled and reminded me it had been a while since I'd eaten anything besides powdered doughnuts and Red Bull.

Fallon's house was a two-story bungalow with peeling paint and a wheelchair ramp to one side of the porch. I rang the doorbell and took a look around while I waited for someone to answer. The grass needed mowing. Neglected hedges bordered the property. By comparison, the neighboring homes were pristine and well maintained. When no one answered the door after a few moments, I knocked.

The door opened a crack with the chain still in place. Fallon peered through the slit, brows furrowed. The harried look on her face morphed into suspicion when she recognized me. "What are you doing here?"

"I'm not stalking you," I said and held up her wallet. "You dropped this at the station."

"Oh. Thanks." Her wariness eased a tiny bit. She closed the door to release the chain then opened it wide enough to claim the wallet.

"No problem." I placed it in her hand. "I opened it to get your address, but I didn't touch anything else. Everything should be in there."

"Okay. Well, thanks again." She tried to close the door when there was a horrific crash from inside the house. "Hank!" She sprinted away, leaving the door wide open.

"Is everything okay?" I lingered at the threshold, unsure if I should go or stay to offer help. A loud bang followed a second crash. Fallon cursed. I made my way over polished hardwood floors into the living room. It took a few seconds for my mind to wrap around the scene in front of me.

The furniture had been pushed to the walls. A hospital bed sat next to the picture window. Rolling shelves held medical supplies. Some type of monitor had been knocked askew. A tray of food lay face down near my feet, its contents strewn over the spotless floor. In the hospital bed, a young man had fallen partially off the mattress, his body bent at an awkward angle. Fallon struggled to right the man.

"Here. Let me help." I stepped forward. "What's his name?"

"Hank," she said breathlessly.

"Hank, I'm Tuck. I'm going to help Fallon get you back on the bed, okay?"

The guy didn't answer, but Fallon nodded, her relief palpable.

"I'll shift his legs," she said and threw the covers aside to reveal the wasted limbs of an invalid.

Together we moved Hank to an upright position. He was a lot heavier than he looked, and it took considerable effort to shift him into place. Fallon transferred into caretaker mode, checking tubes and righting the bedsheets with practiced hands. I backed away to give her access and saw that the guy was young, barely an adult, with the same features as Fallon. Although his body seemed useless, his eyes were a soft, clear topaz, and followed Fallon around the room.

Because I didn't know what else to do, I began to clear the food from the floor. "What should I do with this? Do you have a mop?"

She jumped, as if she'd forgotten I was there. "Um, the food can go in the garbage disposal. And there's a mop next to the sink."

We worked side by side to put the room back together. Fallon talked to the young man, her voice gentle but stern, as she stripped the sheets and changed his clothes. When she was finished, she ran a loving hand through his hair and stroked his cheek. He never replied. An odd pain stabbed my chest at the poignant picture. I cleared my throat and forced my features into neutrality when she faced me.

"Thank you," she said. Lines of exhaustion deepened around her eyes. "I don't know what got into him. He never used to act like this."

"You live alone?" I glanced around the room, at the

worn furniture, the family portraits on the wall. Silence and shadows couched the house.

Fallon took a protective step toward Hank. "That's none of your business."

I sounded like a creepy stalker. I held up a hand. "You're right. I didn't mean to overstep, it's just that he seems like a lot for you to handle on your own." The boy seemed to be around my height, while Fallon barely came to my shoulder. If I had trouble moving him around, it had to be doubly difficult for her.

"It's just the two of us and his live-in nurse. She stays with him while I'm at work, but we're on our own in the evenings." Fallon sank onto the sofa and cradled her head in her hands, her words muffled. "It wasn't so bad when he was younger, but he's grown a lot in the last year."

I couldn't fathom the amount of responsibility resting on her shoulders. She looked much too young to bear such a heavy burden. "Where are your parents?"

"They passed away before—um—Hank's accident. A drunk driver hit them." Her shoulders began to shake. "What am I doing?" she whispered, her voice thick and emotional. "What would've happened if you hadn't come along? I can't do this. It's too much. Too much."

"You would've managed." The slip in her composure touched forced a crack in my stone cold heart. "I'm impressed." I placed my hand on her knee, wanting to comfort her but unsure how it might be perceived from a stranger. She looked skittish, ready to bolt at the first indication of danger.

She lowered her hands and blinked up at me, eyes bright with tears. "Do you think so? I had no idea it would be this difficult when I took custody of him, but I couldn't stick him in a facility. He's all I've got." Her voice broke.

"I'm always terrified that I might do something wrong. I can't leave him alone for even a minute." Tears streamed down her cheeks. "This is impossible."

I pulled her into my arms. Fuck propriety. Her nose nestled in the hollow of my chest, and her fingers clutched my hoodie. I ached for this girl and her brother, for the burdens she carried. "It's okay." I smoothed a hand down her back, feeling the ridges of her spine through the fabric of her blouse. Harsh sobs wracked her body. I let her cry it out until the front of my shirt bore a circle of wetness from her tears. Holding a woman in my arms reminded me how long it had been, and even though the circumstances were less than desirable, it felt good to be strong for someone else, to be needed.

"I'm sorry. I'm not usually a crier." She pushed me away and wiped her eyes with the back of her hand. "I don't— I mean, it's not like me." She cleared her throat and when she spoke again, steel edged her voice. "I appreciate your kindness. Thank you so much."

"No problem. I wish I could do more." We stood up together. I shoved my hands into my pockets. Another minute of watching her cry, and I would have broken down in tears myself or done something inappropriate like kiss her. Both of those things couldn't happen. If I ever released the steel chain guarding my heart, I might never regain the upper hand over my emotions. And I couldn't have that. Not now. Not tonight. Not ever.

7

FALLON

The next morning, I went into work at six to generate Andrew's stupid report. LaTanya, had been kind enough to email the data from her home. I printed the seven pages, placed it on Andrew's desk, then returned to my computer. Because one of the accounts payable clerks had called off, I ran her reports as well, then retrieved a stack of invoices from her desk and began the tedious task of entering the information into the system. It wasn't part of my job description, but because I'd done the job before, worked with efficiency, and could type ninety words per minute, the other supervisors often asked me to assist with their data entry. I didn't mind helping, but I had yet to receive anything more than a cursory nod for my efforts.

In two hours, I finished what would've taken the other girl an entire day. I tapped my pencil on the desk and glanced around. The others wouldn't be in for another thirty minutes. Needing a break, I opened an internet browser and ran a search on Tucker Spaulding. His appearance last night had saved me in a number of ways, first by returning my wallet then helping with Hank. What would I have done without him? The money and credit cards could be replaced, but Hank? My blood ran cold thinking about the possibilities. After years of practice, I could turn and shift him in the bed. A hoist helped move him for bathing and changing, but without Hank's cooperation, the system was useless. He'd gotten heavier and taller over the last year, nearly six feet tall and one hundred thirty pounds. Hillary could manage him on her own, but I was too short and thin to muscle his dead weight without assistance.

I turned back to the search. Tucker's name came up alongside thousands of links. I clicked through the images. He stared back at me, blonder, deeply tanned, snowboarding on a mountain in Switzerland. My pulse quickened at the sight of his large, expressive eyes. I moved through the next pictures. Tucker on a yacht in the Mediterranean with a bevy of bikini-clad beauties around him. Tucker waterskiing. Tucker in the jungles of South America. My favorite was a picture of him sitting alone on the pinnacle of a mountain, surrounded by blue sky, arms clutching his knees to his chest. It was a recent photo, taken less than six months ago.

The photo struck a note within me. On the train, he had seemed so sad, so alone. What had happened to steal the sparkle from his eyes? We had that in common—our sadness. What exactly did it take to make him smile? He'd been full of smiles once. I saw the photos to prove it. When had that changed, and why? I knew why I didn't smile anymore, but what was his story?

Coworkers began to file into their cubicles. I closed the internet browser, putting an end to my cyberstalking. One of the other supervisors approached, and I gritted my teeth. She stopped in front of me and dropped a second stack of invoices onto my desk.

"Mary is getting really behind with these. Could you give us a hand? You're such a dear," she said, and before I could reply, she strode away, leaving me with a mountain of paperwork.

Andrew skulked past my desk. "Hold all my calls," he barked to his assistant. He went straight into his office and shut the door. An hour later, the Vice President of IT arrived. An hour after that, a handful of executives entered the room. Nerves twisted my gut. Eerie silence blanketed the office. The only sounds were the clicking of keyboards and voices as the office snapped into full force.

"What's going on?" I peeked around the wall of my cubicle to Simon's desk.

He peered at me through thick glasses, a flush of bright red racing up his neck, the way it did any time a girl spoke to him. "I dunno. I think they're getting ready to lay off a bunch of people." He tugged at the collar of his plaid shirt with a chubby finger, sending his clip-on tie askew. "One of my friends said they're cutting a hundred jobs in the building. I bet Andrew is shitting."

This tidbit sucked all the moisture from my mouth. Layoffs? I gave Simon a pleasant smile, but inside, my stomach churned and my breakfast threatened to come up. This might not be my dream job, but I needed it. I rolled back to my computer and stared at the screen. What would I do if they let me go? How would I afford Hillary? I stared at the monitor and blinked back a sting of tears. *Don't panic, Fallon. You don't know anything yet.*

For the rest of the day, I kept one eye on Andrew's office

and one eye on the parade of people through his office. At the end of the day, I shut down my computer and resisted the urge to knock on Andrew's door. Better to keep my nose out of the situation than suffer his misdirected wrath. My curiosity would just have to wait.

By the time I arrived home that evening, the responsibility of Hank forced me to put aside the turmoil at work. There were dishes to wash, laundry to put away, menus to plan, meals to cook and freeze for later. My concern for Hank's emotional welfare continued to grow. He no longer wanted to watch TV and refused to eat. He just sat and stared out the window hour after hour, his eyes haunted and empty. Hillary had noticed, too. Her brow furrowed in concern as she prepared to leave.

"He wouldn't eat a thing today," she said from the safety of the kitchen, where we could see him, but he couldn't hear us. "If you ask me, he's depressed again."

"I don't know what to do," I whispered, the words catching in my throat. How could I cheer him up when he had so little to look forward to? I thought about his increasing temper tantrums, his mounting frustrations, the way he'd been acting out. I gave her the short version of the incident from the night before, Tuck's appearance, and how scared I'd been to be alone when Hank had fallen.

"I think you need to talk with his doctor at his next appointment. Maybe he can adjust his antidepressants or get him something different."

"Okay. I will," I said.

She nodded and headed toward the front door. When she opened it, Tuck stood on the other side, a tray of foam cups in one hand and a brown paper bag in the other. My heart skipped a beat then two. Tucker Spaulding was on my doorstep. A ridiculous smile teased my mouth then I glanced down at my tattered sweat pants and drew in a horrified gasp. I needed a shower or, at the very least, a change of clothes.

"Well, hello there," Hillary said. Her assessing gaze lingered over his tall form, the faded jeans hanging low on his hips, and the sexy scruff on his jaw.

"Hi. You must be Hillary. I'm Tuck. I'd shake your hand but—" He glanced at the tray and frowned. "I'm a friend of Fallon's. Is she here?"

"Nice to meet you, Tuck." One of her thick eyebrows lifted as she glanced from Tuck to me. I panicked at the state of my appearance and shook my head. Hillary smiled. Pure mischief glinted in her eyes. "And yes, she's right here. Come on in."

"Hello." I yanked the clip out of my hair and tried to fluff it with my fingers while giving Hillary a murderous glare. Tuck looked relaxed and scrumptious, dirty blond hair mussed and hanging in surfer boy waves to his collar. His gaze dragged over me from head to toe. My nipples tightened beneath my T-shirt. I crossed my arms to hide the way they poked at the cotton fabric. "What are you doing here?"

"Well, I know you can't go out for coffee, so I brought the coffee to you." He pushed the tray toward me. I stood there, staring at it, begging Hillary to rescue me.

"How nice," Hillary said. She maneuvered a shoulder behind mine and gave me a nudge. "The boy's got his hands full. Help him out."

I popped forward and glared at her then smoothed a conscientious hand over my clothes. By the pictures on the internet, this guy had girls fawning all over him, pretty ones. Not that I cared. I took the tray and rested it on the table.

"I wasn't sure what you liked, so I got a couple of different things," he said. "Decaf, latte, cappuccino, black, iced, mocha." He lifted one of six cups to show the descriptions written in ink on the side.

I bit my lip, confused by his thoughtfulness. Wealthy computer geniuses didn't randomly stop by my house to offer coffee. No one stopped by my house—ever.

When I didn't say anything, Tuck continued, "And I wasn't sure about Hank, so I brought a shake for him." He reached in the bag and withdrew two more cups. "Chocolate and vanilla. I hope that's okay."

In the living room, Hank heard his name and turned away from the window for the first time since I'd come home. After a few seconds, his interest waned, and he returned to staring outside at the boys playing football in Neve's yard.

"Oh." The sting of tears bit the back of my eyelids, confusing me even more.

"You'll have to excuse her," Hillary said. Behind Tuck's back, she scowled at me and rolled her eyes. "She's a little socially awkward."

"Yes. I mean, thank you." I stumbled for words to express my gratitude, but nothing else came out.

"Well, I've got to get out of here. Les is waiting for me." Hillary shouldered the strap of her purse then leaned down to my ear. "Pull it together. And, for heaven's sake, be nice."

"I don't have time for this," I muttered through clenched teeth, struggling to keep Tuck from hearing. Meanwhile, my palms continued to sweat.

"Girl, from where I'm standing, you've got nothing but

time," Hillary said, and then she went out the door, closing it behind her, and leaving me alone with Tuck.

While I tried to gather my scrambled wits, Tuck walked into the living room. "Hi, Hank. How's it going?" I watched in shock as he pulled a chair to the side of the bed, rotated it backward, and straddled the seat, leaning his forearms on the backrest.

Hank stared out the window, watching the friendly battle on the lawn.

"He can't talk," I said, spurred into motion by Tuck's interest, hoping to save Hank from embarrassment. "The speech center of his brain sustained serious damage from the accident. He can understand what you're saying. Most of his cognitive abilities are intact." But he wasn't the same. He wasn't the smart-mouthed, intelligent boy I'd grown up with, the one who'd tormented my dates, placed frogs in my shoes, and read my diary out loud to his friends. One reckless act had robbed him of all those things.

"Wow. That's terrible. I'm sorry to hear that." He spoke the words to Hank and not to me. The sincerity in Tuck's tone put a tiny crack in the armor around my heart. "So how does he communicate?"

"We get along." Through experience, I'd come to recognize the blinks and nods of acceptance or displeasure, the low growl of irritation, or the hiss of anger. I brushed a loose lock of hair back from his forehead and made a mental note to find my shears later. He needed a trim in the worst way.

Tuck raised the milkshakes into Hank's line of vision, chocolate on the left and vanilla on the right. "What's your preference, man? Chocolate or vanilla?" Hank's gaze veered to the left. Tuck nodded. "Chocolate it is."

Hank's eyes drifted to mine, seeking permission. Because he got so little exercise, it was important to monitor his diet and prevent weight gain. Now and then, a treat didn't hurt, especially in light of his current hunger strike. I smiled and nodded, happy to see him distracted for even a few minutes. "Okay. But just a little. We'll save the rest for later."

8

TUCKER

The coffee and milkshakes had been an impulse. I didn't stop to think she might be busy or didn't want company. She hadn't been on the train that evening, and even though I tried to dismiss her, I'd been unable to ditch the memory of her large, haunted eyes or the futility of her situation. Everyone deserved a break now and then, and this girl looked like she needed one—big time. Thinking about her and Hank kept my mind off Sydney, and I welcomed the distraction.

After Hank finished his milkshake, he drifted off to sleep. Fallon and I moved to the front porch swing, where a cool evening breeze rustled the leaves. She carried a hand-held monitor, one that allowed her to listen to Hank's breathing from outside the house. We swayed in the twilight, our thighs almost touching. Every time she brushed against me, a thousand tiny fires lit beneath my skin. I resisted the temptation to set my hand on her thigh, because we weren't a couple. Hell, we weren't even friends. I was only there to show kindness to someone in need, nothing more.

"I saw you on the internet," she said after a long and awkward silence. "You're some kind of boy genius, aren't you?"

I shifted in my seat. Statements like that always made me uncomfortable. Being in the limelight had never appealed to me. It was one of the things Sydney and I had never agreed upon, a bone of contention in our relationship. As a reality TV star, she lived for drama and attention, while I preferred to skirt the fringes of anonymity, only coming out to promote my business or favorite charities. "Hardly. I'm thirty years old. And the rest was mainly good timing and luck."

She shook her head. "It takes more than timing and luck to create and sell the most popular video game in history." A spark of something flickered in her eyes. What was it? Curiosity? No, it was more like hunger. "Do you think sometime you could show me some of the code you used? I know it sounds weird, but I'm a total geek when it comes to programming."

This girl never ceased to surprise me. Smart, attractive, and a computer geek, too? I had to admit, she piqued my interest in more than one way. "I could show you now. Where's your computer?"

Two scarlet patches reddened her cheeks. "I don't have a computer anymore."

"What?" My life centered around all things digital. The concept of being unplugged from the virtual world sent my sensibilities into a tailspin.

"I can't afford one. I've had to cut expenses. The cost of internet is exorbitant." Her voice cracked on the admission. "I have a laptop for work and that's it."

"Can't you get some kind of assistance from the government?" Life without internet seemed implausible. The mountain of responsibility resting on her shoulders rendered me speechless. I couldn't imagine living in her shoes for an hour, let alone a day. My respect for her grew with each passing minute.

"Hank receives some government funds, but it doesn't pay for everything. And there have been a lot of cutbacks lately, so he's not getting as much money as before."

"I'm sorry about the interview," I said. She'd come to Twisted Wire looking for better pay, which she desperately needed, and I'd dismissed her efforts. "We gave the job to someone else."

"It's okay." She tucked a strand of hair behind her ear and ducked her head to study the porch floor. "You might as well know, I got into some trouble when I was younger. I'm probably not someone you want working at your business anyway."

"You? Like what?" I prodded. She didn't seem to be the rebellious type. I nudged her sandal with the toe of my tennis shoe. "Did you shoplift candy bars from the convenience store?"

"Uh, no. I hacked into the school mainframe and changed everyone's grades."

I coughed. She pounded my back and waited for me to recover. "Impressive." I could hardly wait to hear the next fascinating surprise to come out of her mouth.

"My parents focused all their attention on Hank, and I think I was acting out to get their attention. Even though he was really young, he was a superstar in Little League baseball. They spent all their time taking him to games and practices and training camps. While they were busy with him, I was busy searching the web." She shrugged and rocked the swing with her toe. "The school administrators wanted to make an example out of me. They charged me with a misdemeanor, and I had to go to juvenile detention. The courts sealed my record, but a lot of people know about it, and it's kept me from getting a better job."

A wave of guilt hit me in the gut. "I'm sorry. I wish I'd known before the interview."

"About what? About me? About Hank?" The fire returned to her eyes, and ignited heat inside me as well. Damn, I liked a spunky woman. "If I'd told you, you'd have hired me out of pity. Is that what you're saying? Well, I don't need your pity, Tucker Spaulding, and neither does Hank." She stood. "Maybe it's time for you to go."

"Whoa. That's not what I meant." I held up my hands, palms facing outward. Me and my big mouth.

"I know your type," she said. Anger stiffened her features. "You're looking for a charity case, someone to soothe your conscience. You think spending five minutes with us will erase your sins. We don't want your handouts."

Was that what I was doing? Using her—them—to ease my guilt? No, that wasn't it at all. I jumped to my feet, angered by her assumption. "I didn't hire you because you weren't the most qualified candidate for the job. There. I said it. Are you happy? It doesn't mean I don't have something else, something you might be perfect for."

Her chin jutted, and she placed a hand on her hip. "Well, I wouldn't work for you now."

A chuckle tickled my throat. My chest vibrated. I swallowed down the laughter, certain she'd miss the humor. She was so damn cute when she was angry. I returned to the swing and patted the cushion beside me. "Okay. I get that. Have a seat, and let's talk about it."

Her eyes narrowed, and she crossed her arms over her chest. "Why are you really here, Tucker? No bullcrap. Straight up."

Damn, this wasn't going to be easy. I wasn't sure myself. I scrubbed a hand over my face and looked across the lawn. How could I explain the long, sleepless nights or the constant self-doubt plaguing my days? I rarely mentioned Sydney's name anymore. I didn't want to be that guy—the one who talked about his ex constantly, begging for sympathy, driving his friends insane. Since arriving at Fallon's, I hadn't thought about Sydney at all until now, but with the subject renewed, the weight of heartache returned.

"I'm not here to save my soul, but if you think you can do it, I'd be grateful." She stared at me, the furrow deepening in her brows. I decided to give her the short, sanitized version. "I've been dealing with some relationship shit. A bad breakup."

Fallon uncrossed her arms and her features relaxed. "I'm sorry, Tucker." The swing jostled as she sat down beside me and placed a hand on my thigh. The heat of her palm burned through my jeans, and something tightened low in my groin. "What a bitch."

"Tell me about it." I blew out a cleansing breath and gathered the strength to continue. "I won't bore you with the details. Let's just say it took me by surprise. It's been three months, and I need to get over it. Being here with you, with Hank, it's the first time I've thought about something other than her. So, yeah, maybe my reasons are selfish. If you still want me to go, I'll understand."

Her gaze roamed over my face, lingering on my eyes, my lips then back to my eyes. My pulse picked up speed. She pressed her lips together. The weight of her hand still rested on my thigh. I liked the way it felt there, calm and reassuring. As if sensing my thoughts, she pulled it into her lap and curled her fingers inward.

"You can stay." The upright square of her shoulders

relaxed, and she leaned back in the swing. "Hank likes you. I haven't seen him show interest in anything in quite a while. I've been worried about his mood. He gets depressed easily. You seemed to help. We don't have a male presence in our lives. I think he needs to have a man around, someone he can relate to."

"So what happened to him?" Maybe it was rude to ask, but I was dying to know more about this girl, how she'd come to be the sole caretaker of her paralyzed brother.

"He went swimming at the quarry with some friends," she said. I knew the place. The rock quarry was a summer hangout for locals, a place for teens to party without surveillance. "They were diving off the cliffs. When it was Hank's turn, he slipped and hit his head on a rock. Twice." She lifted two fingers into the air. "The blow put him off trajectory, and he landed head first in a shallow part of the water. It snapped his neck." Her gaze softened and she stared into the distance. Tears glimmered in her eyes. "I was there with my friends when it happened. I should've been watching him. I should've stopped him."

"You can't blame yourself," I said, but I knew my words held little weight. Of course she blamed herself, and to make up for it, she had devoted her life to his wellbeing. "It was an accident."

"I know." Even though her lips quivered, her voice remained strong. "But it doesn't make it any easier. I keep thinking I could've done something." She shook her head, loose strands of hair floating around her shoulders with the motion. "It's not fair. He's such a sweet kid."

I thought of Hank, lying on the other side of the wall, his promising young life ruined forever by one careless decision. Along with my friends, I'd dived off those cliffs a dozen times and had never considered the danger. It could be me lying paralyzed in a hospital bed instead of him.

"But he can move a little, right?" How else could he have shifted in bed on my first visit? I struggled to understand something I knew so little about.

She nodded. "He's got full movement of his shoulders and some movement in his biceps and pectorals, but no movement in his arms or hands. The brain injury damaged his motor skills, so he doesn't have the ability to learn new ones." She sighed and stared across the dark yard.

My heart went out to this strong girl. Without thinking, I took her hand in mine and squeezed. Small, fragile fingers tightened around mine. A thrill climbed up my arm and into my chest. "So what about you? Do you ever get out of the house? Hang out?"

She stared at me like I'd lost my mind. "This. This is what I do." She raised the monitor in the air with her free hand. The hand inside mine stayed there. Our palms melded together, skin to skin, warm, hers soft, mine rough.

"Oh, come on." I pressed the question.

"I read a lot." By the tension between her brows, she struggled to find an answer. "I don't get much time away from the house." She turned to face me, her amber eyes searching my face with the gravity of someone much older. Blood thundered into my ears, the heat of lust simmering between us. "What about you? What do you do in your spare time?"

"Everything," I said. "I spend a lot of time online, playing video games, and I like sports. I travel when I get a chance, ski, skydive."

"Hank likes sports," she said. Her gaze drifted down to my mouth and hovered on my lips. My dick stirred to life, tempted by her attention. "He watches a lot of baseball in the summer and basketball in the winter."

"Really?" I seized this common thread. "My friend Beckett played college basketball. Maybe he could stop by and see Hank sometime."

"That would be nice," she said. I could tell by her tone she didn't believe me. "He doesn't get any visitors. Not anymore. His friends used to stop by, but now they're busy with their own lives. I think they feel guilty about what happened. I understand, but I'm not sure Hank does."

"That's a shame," I said and meant it. I couldn't imagine a life without friends or family. They were all that had gotten me through the past three months.

Fallon's eyes went to my mouth again. Her tongue glided over her lower lip. An aching need swelled between my ribs. Her body swayed toward me. I leaned forward until the heat of her breath mingled with mine. My heart rate accelerated. We were headed for a kiss, and hell if I didn't want it, looked forward to it, *needed* it.

Tires hissed on pavement. Headlights flashed across the porch. Fallon tensed and pulled away. Hillary waved to us from the driveway.

Fallon dragged her hand out of mine. "I didn't realize it was so late. I've got to get up early tomorrow." She sounded cool, distant. I wasn't sure if I felt disappointed or relieved or a bit angry. It was too soon. My feelings over Sydney were still too raw. The last thing I needed was to get involved with someone, especially someone who seemed more vulnerable than me, whose problems surpassed mine.

"Right." I glanced at my watch. It was almost ten o'clock. I had things to do of my own tomorrow. "I'd better get going."

Her hand brushed my forearm. A jolt of electricity

arced up my arm. She jerked like she'd been bitten. Our eyes met. I swallowed and looked away, unwilling to deal with the pulse of attraction.

"Thank you for the coffee and for Hank," she said. "It was nice to talk."

"No problem." I jogged down the steps and out to the street, eager to escape. Somehow she'd managed to lower my guard, and I'd almost forgotten I was in love with someone else.

9

FALLON

On Saturday, I looked forward to a day of cleaning, laundry, and yard work. If I wasn't too exhausted later, I might tackle the jungle of overgrown hedges. Hillary had the weekends off, and I wanted to be dressed and ready when the caregiver arrived from the agency. They usually sent one of the same three people, but sometimes, like today, I had an alternate, someone unfamiliar with Hank's routine. Change always made me uneasy.

When the doorbell rang, I trotted to the door. My heart did a ridiculous dance at the sight of Tuck on the front porch. He seemed taller, and I had to tilt my head to see his face. Morning sunlight slanted across the bill of his baseball cap and shadowed his eyes. I never expected to see him again after Tuesday night. People didn't like visiting our house. I think Hank's injuries reminded them of their mortality or made them feel guilty for their own healthy bodies.

"Hey," I said. Lamest greeting ever. I tried not to stare at the bulge of biceps below his shirtsleeves or the thick veins running down his forearms. *Swoon.*

The memory of our *almost* kiss played through my head. Except, in my daydreams, he'd pulled me into his strong arms, bent me backward, and ravaged my mouth. I'd been reliving the moment with pathetic frequency until I'd convinced myself it was a figment of my imagination. Hot, sexy millionaires didn't make out with plain, worn-out girls like me. But seeing him on my stoop made me question all of my convictions.

"I hope it's not too early. We thought we'd come and help you with your yard work." Behind him, parked by the street, was a pickup truck filled with landscape equipment.

He gestured to a guy with sandy brown hair, leaning on a push lawnmower. The guy lifted a hand in a shy wave. "That's Caleb."

I opened my mouth to protest at the same time the new caregiver pulled into the driveway. "I appreciate the thought, but it's not—" A short woman with frizzy, unkempt hair and mismatched scrubs meandered up the sidewalk toward us. Her unprofessional appearance raised a number of warning flags. I lifted a finger to Tuck. "I'm sorry, could you give me a minute?"

He nodded and donned a pair of black sunglasses to hide his eyes. "Sure. Take your time. We'll go ahead and get started."

After a brief introduction, the woman followed me into the house. As I took her to Hank's bedside, she regaled me with stories of her aching back, chronic fatigue syndrome, and aversion to bodily fluids. I bit my lower lip to hold back the sharp words on the tip of my tongue.

"And I don't cook or clean," she added.

"Would you excuse me for a second?" I asked. "I need

to make a phone call." *Stay calm, be professional.* In the next room, I dialed the agency.

"I'm sorry, but we don't have anyone else," the manager said when I requested a new person.

"You can't be serious." I closed my eyes and pinched the bridge of my nose. "What about Misty, or Leroy? Is one of them available?"

"I'm sorry, Miss Youngblood, but there's no one else," the manager said, his patience obviously thinning.

I hung up the phone and tried not to have a meltdown. I couldn't manage Hank alone for an entire day. My only choice was to stay close and power through the situation. The household chores would have to wait for another day.

The buzz of the lawnmower distracted me. I glanced out the living room window to see Tuck and Caleb in the yard. In my stress, I'd forgotten about them, but they were already hard at work. Their friendly banter carried through the open window. Tuck had removed his shirt. Sweat glistened on his tan, bare chest as he trimmed the hedge between our yard and the neighbor's. The waist of his jeans hung low enough to reveal a sharp cut of muscle on each hip. I paused to admire the sight of a handsome, half-naked guy doing manual labor in my yard. At my sides, my fingers curled into fists, overcome with the desire to run my hands over the rippling six-pack of his abs. I allowed myself the fantasy, wondering if his skin would be hot to the touch, how his sweat might smell.

From the yard next door, Neve noticed Tucker, too, and my fantasy ground to a screeching halt. She and a few of her bikini-clad friends lounged on blankets in the grass. When Tuck moved to the hedge separating the two properties, Neve bounced over to the hedge, twirling a strand of hair between her fingertips. One side of his mouth lifted in appreciation. At seventeen, she was too young for him, but I still felt a prickle of jealousy. I ran a hand over my plain gray T-shirt and baggy sweatpants. Beside me, Hank watched the interaction. He bit his lower lip, eyes darkening. From the recliner at his side, the caregiver snored, oblivious to either of us.

"I'll be back," I told him and patted his cheek. I took the stairs two at a time to my bedroom. After rummaging through the meager contents of my closet, I pulled on a pair of navy blue shorts and a polka dot swing top. The high waist made my boobs appear twice as big. I dabbed on a bit of mascara and lip gloss then swept my hair into a clip, filled with an inexplicable need to impress Tucker. I blamed it on my competitive streak, the one I'd managed to repress for the past three years, but it was more than that. I wanted him to notice me, to look at me the way he looked at Neve. Like I mattered to him.

Yesterday, I'd made fresh lemonade. In the kitchen, I garnished the rim of two glasses with sugar and a slice of lemon. I carried the refreshments on a tray into the yard. Tuck heard the door swing shut behind me and left Neve without a backward glance.

"This is great," he said after a deep drink. "Did you make this?" A few grains of sugar clung to his lip. He swiped them away with his tongue. I held back a groan at the sensual display.

"Yes," I said, like a fawning teenager, desperate for his approval. "It's Hank's favorite."

"Tasty stuff." Caleb downed his glass and replaced it on the tray. I liked his soft brown eyes and shy smile. "Thanks." He returned to the mower, but Tuck stayed at my side.

"The yard—it looks nice," I said. Butterflies tumbled around inside my stomach. "I can't thank you enough."

"Yeah? No problem." For the first time since I'd known him, Tuck smiled. The brilliance of his white teeth and the lone dimple in his cheek stole my breath. It slipped away as quickly as it appeared. My traitorous eyes went straight to his mouth and stayed there, wondering if his lips were as soft as they appeared. *Look away, Fallon.* I dropped my gaze and it landed on the bulge behind the faded zipper of his jeans. *No, shit. Not there.* I cleared my throat and blew out a breath before returning my focus to the equally dangerous but socially acceptable area of his eyes.

"You seem to know your way around a yard," I said, floundering for conversation, flustered by the proximity of his flexing muscles. I bet he knew his way around a woman's body as well. Geez. What was wrong with me? I was worse than a cat in heat. Oh, who was I kidding? I *was* in heat. Serious, earth-scorching, center-of-the-sun heat.

"I spent a lot of time mowing yards as a kid," he said. Once he'd finished his lemonade, he put the glass back on the tray and took it from me. Thank God, because my hands trembled until the glasses rattled. "Let me carry this inside for you. Do you mind if I use your restroom?"

"Sure. Come on in." I'd been away from Hank too long and gladly led the way inside the house. My heart pounded with absurd speed when Tuck's bare shoulder brushed my arm as we squeezed through the doorway.

I went to the kitchen and put the tray away then washed the glasses. A few minutes later, I heard Tuck's voice in the living room. He stood next to Hank's bed. Both of them stared out the window, where Neve and her girl-friends paraded around in their tiny bikinis.

"Can't say I blame you there, man," Tuck said. "She's a pretty girl." A feeling of warmth crawled up my body at the way he talked to Hank, like he was a person, like he understood. "But let me tell you a little secret. Girls like her are nothing but heartache." Hank searched Tuck's face, eyes round. "Ah, so you know what I'm talking about, right?" Hank blinked, and Tuck nodded. "You're better off to stay away from chicks like her."

The sight of Hank interacting with another person, a virtual stranger, brought the blur of tears to my eyes. I placed a hand over my heart, too overwhelmed to do anything more than stand and observe the miracle.

"Yeah, she's bad news. You need a good woman. Someone like your sister."

Hank rolled his eyes, and Tuck laughed. I liked the sound of his laughter, the deep rumble of it, the way it seemed to start in his chest and bubbled up to his lips.

From her seat in the recliner next to Hank's bed, the caregiver gave a snort. She'd been fast asleep for the better part of an hour. Tuck looked over at her and gave the base of the chair a sharp kick. She jerked awake, eyes wide with alarm. I pressed a hand to my mouth to suppress a laugh.

"What? What is it?" The woman popped out of the chair.

"Shouldn't you be doing something besides sleeping?" Tuck asked her. Ice coated his words.

"What I do is none of your business," she said, but she began tidying Hank's covers. "I don't work for you."

A muscle ticked in Tuck's jaw. He glanced up, spied me standing in the doorway, and crossed the room. He took my elbow and backed us into the hallway. "What's the deal with this woman, anyway?" The amount of anger in his voice caught me off guard. His proximity violated my personal space. The heat of his body sent a wave of goose-flesh up my arms.

I cleared my throat and pushed aside the attraction. "I

know. She sucks, huh? The service didn't have anyone else to send."

He shoved a hand through the mess of his hair. "She needs to go. Send her home."

The man had clearly lost his mind. "I can't just send her home. Are you crazy? I need someone here." I could handle most of Hank's duties by myself, but a second person meant Hank never had to go unattended for even a minute. A warm body was better than no help at all.

"I'll stay." Intensity swirled in his eyes. These two simple words blew me away. I gawked at him, certain his mind had derailed. No one in their right mind would volunteer for this kind of responsibility. He crossed his arms over his chest and braced his legs. "You don't need someone like her."

Even though I agreed with him, his statement put me on the defensive, and I mimicked his stance. I was constantly second-guessing my efforts, my decisions, my capability to do this job. "Do you have any idea how difficult it is to care for Hank? The amount of time involved in the simplest things? He can't do anything for himself. Nothing. He can't go to the bathroom, brush his teeth, get dressed, blow his nose."

"Maybe I'm not trained, but I'm a damn sight better than that." He jerked a thumb toward the caregiver, who'd nodded off in the recliner again.

All the frustration and anger from the past few years drew to a boil and unleashed on Tuck. "It's easy for you to judge. You've been here, what? Five minutes?" Bitter tears stung my eyes. I blinked them back. "You have no idea. I'm doing the best I can."

"Hey, hey." Strong arms circled my shoulders and drew me into his naked chest. I stiffened, unused to the physical contact, shocked by the heat of his bare skin against my cheek. No one other than Hillary had hugged me since my parents' funeral. "I'm Team Fallon, all the way. You don't have to explain yourself. I think you're doing a fantastic job here."

One of his hands stroked the back of my head. My nose nestled just above the leather thong around his neck. I drew in the scent of his soap and his skin, the musk of male sweat. It was too easy to imagine lying on his chest after a heady session of lovemaking, listening to the steady thump of his heart, feeling the rhythmic rise and fall of his ribs with each breath. Those were dangerous thoughts, ones I shouldn't have, but I couldn't help myself.

"Sometimes it's too much," I whispered into his neck. "I'm going nuts."

"You're not nuts. You're doing what needs to be done, and doing a kick-ass job of it," he murmured in my hair. A rush of needs, desires, conflicted my thoughts. I wanted to push him away, to tug him closer, to sink deeper into his embrace, to press hot kisses along his collarbone. I exhaled and tried to relax, to remember not everyone was out to get me, but I'd been burned too many times by the people who should've had my back.

"Tuck?" Caleb knocked on the door.

Tuck and I stiffened. We'd both been caught unguarded. I saw the realization in his eyes as his arms dropped, a gentle storm of unspoken thoughts swirling in his eyes.

"Come in," I said, unable to look away from Tuck.

"What's up?" Tuck stared back at me, his confusion obvious by the slant of his brows. Did he feel it, too—this insane want?

"The belt broke on the mower. I'm going to run to the

parts store and get another one." Caleb joined us in the hall-way. It had been a long time since I'd had such an overpow-ering male presence in the house. Their testosterone filled the narrow space.

"Okay. Go ahead. I'm going to hang out here," Tuck said. He looked away, snapping the invisible line between us. "Hey, before you go, I want you to meet Hank. If that's okay, Fallon?"

"Sure," I said.

Caleb squatted down next to Hank's bed, lowering himself to his eye level. "Hank. I'm Caleb. Tuck's told me a lot about you. Nice to meet you."

Tuck placed a hand on Caleb's shoulder. "Hank, Caleb's my wingman."

Caleb snorted and shot Tuck a playful, disdainful glance over his shoulder. "You wish." He returned his atten-tion to Hank. My brother watched the two men with a light of sharp interest in his eyes. The first I'd seen since the acci-dent. "Don't let him fool you. If anyone's the wingman, it's Tuck." He waggled an eyebrow. "The ladies flock to me."

"Oh, get out." Tuck gave Caleb a mock glare. And then something miraculous happened, something so unexpected and wholly wonderful, that it stole my breath.

Hank smiled.

10

____

TUCKER

Fallon sent away the lazy-ass caregiver. I walked the woman to her car, ignoring her grumbles and complaints, and vowed to give the agency a call later to let them know exactly what I thought of their hiring practices. Once she was gone, Caleb finished the yard, and Fallon and I devoted the rest of the afternoon to Hank's needs. When she'd said I had no idea the amount of work involved in caring for Hank, she hadn't been exaggerating. She had to turn him every two hours. Because he couldn't cough, she massaged and pounded on his chest to clear the phlegm. Hank endured the indignities, but I saw the frustration and anger in his eyes. I felt those emotions for him, wanted to scream on his behalf, but I didn't. Instead, I watched Fallon's tireless devotion, her infinite compassion, and it impressed me beyond words.

After Hank ate dinner, Fallon stripped away his clothes and tucked him in to sleep. When his eyes drifted shut, we moved outside to the porch swing, where it was cooler. Except for the cars leaving and going from Neve's driveway, a calm quiet prevailed throughout the neighborhood. I liked it here, the serenity of the street and the occasional snippets of laughter floating from the neighboring homes.

"Damn, girl," I said, feeling the heaviness of my own eyelids. "I don't know how you do it. I'm exhausted."

"That's nothing," she said with a wave of her hand. Weariness etched her features. "It takes at least three hours to get him ready each morning. And whenever he goes to the doctor, you're looking at an entire day."

"How do you get him there?" During the course of the afternoon, I'd noticed the absence of a vehicle in the driveway, and Hillary's compact certainly wasn't equipped to transport a handicapped person.

"Angels on Wheels provides transportation." The chain of the swing squeaked as we rocked back and forth and the scent of steaks on the grill wafted across the yard.

"But what about fun stuff? I mean, how long since he's been anywhere other than the hospital or the doctor?" I couldn't imagine a lifetime confined to the same four walls, the same tiny space.

She frowned, and her defensive tone suggested I'd touched on a sore subject. "He's never been anywhere else since the accident. I can't manage him on my own. And his wheelchair's not the best."

Silence stretched between us. I'd been lucky enough to travel the world, to see some of the most beautiful places on Earth. Too long in one spot and I began to go crazy. My chest ached at the thought of being seventeen and locked inside, even on a beautiful night like this one, with no hope of escape.

"What if you could change that?" I didn't want to give her false hope, but there had to be a way. Ideas began to tumble through my head. "What if you had an opportunity to get him out of the house? It might help."

She rested a hand on my arm. I stared at the place where she touched me, where her delicate fingers splayed, where fire ignited beneath my skin. "I appreciate the thought, but we're not your problem to solve."

Our conversation ended when a group of teenagers flocked across the lawn from Neve's house. They stopped at the base of the porch. Three boys about the same age as Hank jostled each other for position while Neve hung back with two of her girlfriends. Beside me, Fallon braced as if preparing for an attack.

"Hey, man." The tallest one, the apparent ringleader, spoke first.

"Hey, what's up?" I asked.

"Hi, Jimmy," Fallon said. "How are you?"

"Fine, thanks," he replied. His gaze drifted back to me, and I knew where the conversation was heading before he spoke. "I'm sorry to bother you, but aren't you Tucker Spaulding?"

I nodded.

The boy behind Jimmy gave him a small shove. "See, man. I told you."

"*Dragons of Destiny* is the best game ever," Jimmy exclaimed.

"Thanks. Glad you like it."

"Can you tell me how to get to level twenty?" asked one of the others. "I'm stuck."

"Yeah, that's a hard one." I tried to look sympathetic. After all, kids like them were my meal ticket. "I'd love to help you out, but some other time, alright? I'm hanging with Fallon and Hank tonight."

"Oh, okay." A murmur of disappointment rippled through the group. They turned away as a unit, all except Neve.

"How is Hank?" Neve stepped forward and spoke in a soft, shy voice. She was curvy and blond with long-lashed blue eyes and a mole above the left side of her mouth. I could see why Hank was fascinated with her. She had a California girl, wholesome appeal. Hell, if I was seventeen, I'd be fascinated, too.

"He's good," Fallon replied. I felt her body relax next to mine.

"Would you tell him I said hi?" Neve asked.

"Sure," Fallon said. I heard the note of disappointment in her voice.

"You could tell him yourself," I said.

"Okay. Maybe," Neve replied.

The others called to her, summoning her away. She hesitated, lips pursed as if to say more, then moved toward the group with a wave. For the next hour, their laughter drifted across the driveway while Fallon and I sat in comfortable silence. She and Hank lived a complicated life, struggling to meet their most basic needs. The contrast between the frolicking teens and the boy on the bed filled me with a burning frustration, one that followed me throughout the night and haunted my thoughts well into the next day.

11

———

FALLON

On Monday, my attention kept veering away from work and back to Tucker. While I ran the morning reports for Andrew, I doodled Tuck's name in the margins of my notepad. *Tuck. Tucker. Tucker Spaulding. Mrs. Tucker Spaulding. Fallon Spaulding.* When I realized what I'd done, I gasped in horror and scribbled out all evidence of my insanity. What was I thinking? We weren't dating. We weren't anything.

Our relationship needed to remain in the friend zone, but memories of his naked chest, sweat gleaming on his rippling six-pack, and the way his jeans draped over his delectable ass, kept my panties damp. I twitched my thighs together and swallowed back a groan of sexual frustration. His smooth southern drawl echoed in my ears, the liquid slide of vowels over his tongue, the way he pressed his lips together before he spoke. I closed my eyes, imagining the clean scent of his shampoo against the backdrop of fresh cut grass. In my daydream, I begged him to have his way with me, to ravage me. *Kiss me, Tucker.* His fingers fisted in my ponytail, jerking my mouth to his—

"Did you say something?" Simon put an abrupt halt to my daydream.

Fire erupted in the tips of my ears. I opened my eyes to find him peering around the edge of our shared cubicle wall. "Um, no." I snatched up a stack of papers, pretending to sort and organize them. "I was on the phone." I flicked on the small, personal fan at my desk and tried to regroup. What the heck was wrong with me?

"Oh, okay." Simon shoved his glasses up his nose. "Something's going on." He nodded toward Andrew's closed door then disappeared into his cubicle.

The head of Human Resources, an intimidating woman in a severe black suit, entered the room and went straight to Andrew's office. Nervous energy thickened the air. A few minutes later, two members of security stood watch outside the door. My palms began to sweat. Andrew opened the door and called out someone's name. One by one, he took my coworkers into his office and one by one, they were escorted out of the building by security until only a handful of people remained.

"Ms. Youngblood, can I see you in my office?"

I flinched at the sound of Andrew's nasal voice. He loved to sneak up on me. I hated our cubicle desks. The design forced us to sit with our backs to the flow of traffic, making it impossible to see someone approach.

"Sure." I crumpled the paper with Tucker's name on it, shoved the sheet into the shred bin, and followed him to his office. My heart rattled between my ribs. The past week had been tense as a litany of executives had paraded through the department. The company had yet to address the situation with the workers. Their lack of comment concerned me on a number of levels. I didn't like being in the dark, especially when my financial future was at stake.

I took a seat in front of Andrew's desk and waited. The HR Director had left the room, a good sign. At least he didn't intend to let me go. I bit the inside of my cheek and braced for the news. I never knew when or if he was going to start yelling, which way his mood might swing. I hoped it was good news, because today might be the day I yelled back at him. My quick temper had always been a weakness, and I'd been swallowing down frustration for weeks. Hank's accident, dealing with his needs, had forced me to learn control, but tiny fissures had begun to weaken the walls around my emotions. My little crying jag after Hank's fall had been a precursor to an impending meltdown.

"I need more from you." Andrew launched into his attack without preamble. I exhaled through my nose. "I'm sure you've noticed the scrutiny around our department. The company is undergoing changes. Your duties are going to increase. I need you to step up, take on more responsibility." He rested his fingers on the desktop and steepled his fingers in front of him.

Was he serious? I stared at him, jaw slack. "What do you mean, *changes?*" Change scared me. I liked safe, routine, normal. Seeing my coworkers dismissed without warning had been more than enough change for one day.

"We're going to implement a reduction in workforce—a reorganization. You will assume the duties of my assistant as well as continuing your work as group lead. I'll need you to come in earlier, stay later. You'll need to pick up the slack as we streamline the department. It's a lot of responsibility, but I know you're up for the task." He sat back in his chair and waited for my response, a smug smile on his thin lips, like he was doing me a favor.

Angry heat started in my chest and climbed into my face. I'd been working up the nerve to ask for a raise. *More responsibility. Stay later. Come in earlier.* The words replayed in a loop inside my head. I continued to take on more work and had gotten nothing for it—not even a thank you. *More. Later. Earlier.* I counted to ten before I spoke. "I assume there will be a pay increase in alignment with the shift in responsibilities."

"The company isn't in a position to offer you additional pay." The cool unconcern on his face ignited my temper. "But this is a good opportunity for you to show your dedication to Reyes Media. You'll gain experience. Your help will be greatly appreciated. You're an invaluable member of our team here. And, if a position opens up and you'd like to apply, we'll be happy to consider you."

"So I'm invaluable, but not enough for a raise? I already do the work of three people." I lifted an eyebrow, unable to hold back the bitter sarcasm. My voice circumvented my brain and spoke without my permission. "No thanks. I'll stay where I'm at."

"Ms. Youngblood, you should have no expectation of promotion or monetary compensation for these additional duties. We've made you no promises. What I'm offering here is a privilege. We recognize your potential and would like to reward you with the opportunity for growth, to learn, to sharpen your skills. I'm sure there are a dozen people in this department who'd jump at the chance I'm offering here."

I stood. "I'm happy to take on the extra responsibility, but I expect to be compensated accordingly." I'd been silent for so long, the release felt good. Part of me wavered, unwilling to risk my job. The rebellious part of me, the one I'd suppressed since Hank's accident, jumped headlong into the fire. "I'm already filling in for the payables supervisor." I'd been doing her job for almost three months while she recovered from a heart attack, probably caused by the stress of her position.

Andrew slapped a hand on his desk. His voice shook with anger. "I don't like your attitude, Ms. Youngblood. You don't seem to understand. This isn't optional. You've already been assigned the work, and the changes are being implemented as we speak." I shook my head and moved toward the door, afraid I'd burst into flame if I stayed any longer. "Ms. Youngblood! We're not finished here."

I kept walking and let the door bang shut behind me. Curious eyes peered over cubicle walls. I avoided their gazes and returned to my desk. Judging by the silence in the workspace, they'd heard every word of the conversation. My knees gave out as I sank into my chair. What had I done? I needed this job. I couldn't afford to be unemployed. What if Andrew decided to let me go next?

12

TUCKER

Twisted Wire Productions, was the fruition of all my fantasies. Through hard work and a lucky twist of fate, I'd designed the bestselling video game of all time. Once I'd sold the movie rights to my first game, I had a bank account full of money. Six months later, I'd opened my own company in a nice office building. I'd had the space specially designed for my creative team, one they jokingly referred to as the Inner Sanctum. This was where we came to think, dream, and blow off steam. The large room boasted beanbag chairs, video game consoles, floor-to-ceiling flat screen monitors, and a wet bar along the far wall. Heavy metal music reverberated through the open space. We were supposed to be brainstorming ideas for a new game. Well, they were brainstorming. My attention was elsewhere, centering on a certain brown-haired girl and her sweet-faced brother.

"Dude, what's with you?" Caleb propped his feet on the desk, legs crossed at the ankle. A dark blue bandana circled his head in an attempt to tame the mop of his hair. Roni, my game mechanics designer, lay on her back atop her desk and bounced a tennis ball off of the ceiling. Upon hearing Caleb's question, she stopped throwing the ball. They both turned to stare at me.

"What?" I asked. I'd only been half listening, absorbed in a Google search for state-of-the-art wheelchairs.

"You've smiled twice today." He narrowed his eyes. "Who are you, and what have you done with Tucker?"

"You're, like, obsessed with this kid," Roni said, leaning over to steal a peek at my computer screen.

I hit a key and flipped the display to my screensaver.

Caleb snorted. "It's not the kid he's obsessed with."

"Shut up," I said. The heat of embarrassment crawled up my neck.

"Wait. Don't tell me." Roni swung her feet to the floor and sat up, features alight with interest. "There's a girl in this story?" When I ignored her, she turned to Caleb for confirmation.

"Not just a girl. A pretty, smart girl." Caleb nodded, a sly smirk on his lips. "Tuck's in love."

Even though he was teasing, his words sent me into a panic. The walls of my chest tightened. I didn't do love. "Don't go there," I said. The smile dropped off his face when he saw my warning glare. "Can't a guy help someone without being accused of all kinds of crazy shit?"

Roni and Caleb exchanged a look, suggesting neither of them believed my protests.

"He's been mowing her lawn," Caleb said, his tone droll. "He doesn't mow his own lawn, let alone someone else's."

"Wow." Roni lifted her hands, eyes wide.

"You say you're not into her, but you haven't stopped talking about her." A knowing smile brightened his round face.

"It's not like that. She needs help, and so does Hank." I flipped my middle finger at him then returned my focus back to the computer and scrolled through the links. "You were there. You saw how it is."

Caleb stood and came around to my side. "What have you found?" His genuine interest and sincerity soothed my irritation.

"There's some seriously cool stuff on here. Look at this one." I pointed to a picture of an electric wheelchair operated by a paraplegic through the use of a mouthpiece. "Something like this would be perfect for him."

In the news feed on the right side of my screen, something—some*one*—caught my eye. Black hair, red lips, a brilliant smile. My heart stuttered and stopped. Sydney. Caleb caught sight of the picture at the same time. I stared at the photograph of Sydney and her new husband. She wore a form-fitting white dress, the enormous train fanned in a circle behind her. At her side stood Alex, the Australian actor, the one who'd stolen my girl. Except she wasn't my girl. She was his wife. And, if this particular headline was true, having his baby.

Caleb slammed the laptop shut, almost clipping my fingers in the process. I stared at the desk. A sickening knot tightened in my gut. How could I have fallen so hard and so deeply in love with someone who didn't love me back? How did I miss the signs? My mind raced through memories, desperate for clues to prove I hadn't been wrong, that some part of her had cared for me. Every touch, every kiss, every caress seemed tainted. I'd fallen for her charade like a fool.

I pushed away from the desk. The walls of the room closed in around me until my lungs struggled for breath. I stalked out of the office. Caleb and Roni stared after me, foreheads puckered. I hated their pity almost as much as I hated my own. The door slammed shut on my heels. A few seconds later, it opened, and Caleb followed me into the hall. I forced an expression of apathy onto my face and let numbness chase away the anger and hurt choking me.

"You okay?" he asked.

I avoided his worried gaze and stared out the large window overlooking the street. Beyond the glass, heat shimmered over the asphalt, and people milled along the sidewalks. "I'm fine. It's fine."

Caleb shoved his hands in his pockets and leaned on the wall behind us. The weight of his gaze burned into me. "Look, I know you really liked that chick, but honestly, I never understood the pull. Sure, she's hot, but if you ask me, you're better off without her. She chose fame over love, and that's fucked up. In your heart, you know she wasn't right for you."

In spite of the heat outside, an icy chill filled my chest. I faced Caleb. "I'm good. I'm over it." I smiled. The skin of my cheeks pulled tight at the unnatural act. "It was just a shock, that's all." I shrugged and clapped him on the arm. "No worries. She's moved on. I'm moving on."

Caleb relaxed, his shoulders dropping. Apparently, Sydney wasn't the only talented actor, because Caleb seemed to believe my charade. I'm not sure who I wanted to convince more—him or myself. Even though I appeared okay, my insides churned. I turned back to the window. My gaze fell on the tall, taunting spires of Seaforth Towers in the skyscape. There was only one thing that could chase away the angst, the emptiness. A sense of purpose replaced the ache. I straightened, my mind snapping with excitement.

"Let's do it." I turned to Caleb. His eyes brightened. "Call your friend."

"Seriously?" A smile lit his face. He fist-pumped the air. "Yes."

A few days later, from the roof of the Seaforth Towers, I could see the entire city, the colors bright and crisp. Laurel Lake sparkled like a blue diamond in the distance. I drew in a deep lungful of air and tried to quiet my racing pulse. For the first time in weeks, I felt alive. I had purpose.

"I'm here, man," I said into the Bluetooth hooked over my ear.

"About time," replied Caleb. "I've been waiting forever."

"Sorry. My interview ran late, and I had a little trouble getting up to the roof." Without further delay, I climbed into my gear and began the safety check, tightening straps and testing buckles.

"Why do you bother with those interviews?" Caleb asked, irritation clear in his voice. "You have people to do that for you. You're the freaking CEO."

"I'm never going to be one of those corporate assholes who doesn't know the people working for him." I tipped my head back and studied the blue sky. Fluffy clouds billowed overhead, peaceful and solemn. Their serenity calmed the unrest in my soul. I closed my eyes, drew in a deep breath, and relished the rush of fresh air into my lungs.

"Yeah, yeah. Whatever." Static blurred his voice then cleared. "You ready to make this building your bitch?"

"Hell yeah." Was I ever. Nothing put my life into perspective more than a brush with death. The element of danger got my blood pumping, cleared my head, and infused new life into my soul.

"Stellar," Caleb said. "The wind is three miles per hour

out of the east. You've got a perfect shot from the south side. Just like we planned." Caleb's van sat in a parking lot at the end of the block. From his station, he had a clear view of the street and building.

I climbed over the security rail and wandered onto the flat part of the roof. We'd put a lot of careful planning into this day, and I didn't want to fuck anything up. If something went wrong, I wouldn't get another chance. The idea of personal harm never crossed my mind. I just didn't want to get caught. City ordinances prohibited BASE jumping within the city limits, and I had no desire to spend the night in jail. After a deep breath, I inched to the edge of the roof and glanced down. For a brief moment, the distance to the ground spun my head. I swallowed and closed my eyes.

One deep breath, then two. Blood pounded through my arteries and veins. The chambers of my heart kicked against my ribs. For the first time in weeks, months, I felt alive. Every nerve, muscle, and fiber in my being resonated with excitement. I jumped. Time stopped. A bizarre sense of calm hijacked my senses. For one blissful moment, my problems fell away. A thousand thoughts raced through my head. Was this how it felt to die? This sickening, euphoric rush of adrenalin as the ground raced to meet me? I chased the feeling—the sensation of weightless freedom—like a junkie chased his next fix. Anything to drive away the memory of the girl who'd broken my heart.

The sun had reached its highest point in the sky when we arrived back at the office. I'd barely evaded the cops and spent the better part of an hour hiding in a Dumpster outside a Chinese restaurant. Roni sprawled over an armchair, controller in hand, pounding the hell out of our latest test game. The short purple pikes of her hair vibrated every time she yanked the controller—which was a lot. When the door closed behind me, she took one look at my soiled clothing, pinched her nose shut with thumb and forefinger, and pointed toward the men's room.

I grabbed a change of clothes from the closet. Caleb followed me into the restroom. When the door swung shut behind us, he shoved me into the wall with two hands on my chest. "You crazy motherfucker. If you ever do something stupid like that again, I'll kick your ass."

"Chill. Everything's fine." While he glowered, I peeled out of my shirt, sniffed it then tossed it into the trash can. "The cops never saw me. It's cool."

"That's not what I meant, and you know it." He blew out a heavy breath and leaned against the wall, arms crossed over his chest. I turned on the shower, stripped out of the remainder of my clothing. "You're cutting it too close, man. One of these times you're going end up *splat* on the sidewalk." He clapped his hands together to emphasize the point. I winced.

He was right. I couldn't deny it. Since Sydney had dumped me, I'd been lax about my personal safety, taunting death, toeing the line between reckless and crazy, taking more and more risks. Those few moments of insanity were the only times I felt alive. The rest of the time, I existed in a fog of numbness, feeling nothing, not even regret, just —*nothing*.

"You talk like my grandma."

"I've got half a mind to tell your grandma. I know for sure she'll kick your ass." He scrubbed both hands over his face and began to pace the length of the room with heavy footsteps. "You waited too long to throw your chute. It's like

—like—" He stumbled for words, too furious to be fluent. "It's like you *wanted* to die."

"Don't be stupid." I pushed past him, but he blocked my path.

"Is that what you want? Do you just not care anymore?"

We glared at each other. After a prolonged silence, I shouldered around him and into the shower stall. The rush of hot water drowned out his lecture and rinsed away the stench of the Dumpster but did nothing for the pain. Had I gone too far? Was I out of control? Safety played a huge part of any sport. Although I enjoyed the challenge of BASE jumping, the risk of personal injury or even death always loomed in the background. One wrong move, one tiny oversight, could end a person's life. I'd seen it happen to one of our friends. It could have happened to Hank. I leaned my forehead against the shower wall and let the steaming water run over my neck and shoulders.

Outside the shower, fog clouded the mirror over the sink. I used the side of my fist to wipe it away and stared at my face. A stranger stared back at me, eyes wild, hair tumbled, and two day's growth of beard on his cheeks. Who was this man? I scrubbed my face with the towel and pulled on my clothes. Was Caleb right? Had I lost my mind? Once the thrill of today's jump faded, emptiness swelled inside me, larger and colder than ever. I couldn't go on like this, running from a past I couldn't change, hiding from pain I didn't want to face.

13
____

FALLON

Sometimes I saw Tuck on the train before or after work. Every morning, I donned my best clothes, added lip gloss and mascara to my cosmetic routine, and paid particular attention to my hair. Tuesdays became his regular night to stop by the house. After work, I raced home to change clothes and freshen my makeup before he arrived, all to the great amusement of Hillary. He usually brought an armload of food as well as some kind of gift for Hank, a DVD, or an audiobook. On Saturdays, he mowed the yard, often accompanied by Caleb and one or more of their friends. I looked forward to his visits, for Hank's sake, I told myself. In reality, I enjoyed Tuck's company, his easygoing demeanor, his slow southern drawl, and the way he could sit for hours without saying anything.

On this particular Saturday, a month after his first visit, Tuck knocked on the door and came inside. My heart raced at the sight of him, dressed in his usual T-shirt and jeans. He seemed comfortable in my house, oblivious to the clutter of medical supplies and equipment. While I trimmed Hank's hair, Tuck dragged a chair to his bedside and turned it backward to observe. Our eyes met over the top of my brother's head, and blood heated my cheeks.

"I was talking with Hank the other day, and we thought maybe we could watch the game together next Saturday," he said. "Just a few friends."

"So you two have been conspiring behind my back." I brushed the loose hairs from Hank's forehead, unable to repress a smile. I loved the way Tuck included him in his conversations. I waved my scissors around the room. "Here? In this house?"

"Sure. Just a few of my friends. Nice people. They'll love Hank, and he'll love them."

"I don't know." I ran my fingers through Hank's hair to gauge the length then gave him a kiss on the top of his head. "I don't really have time to cook and clean up after a bunch of people." It had been a long time since anyone other than Tuck had visited our home. The idea of strangers in my safe zone made my palms sweat. "And I don't want to tire Hank out. He's not used to a lot of excitement."

"I think it's a great idea," Hillary said from the kitchen. Les had gone out of town on business for the weekend, so she'd chosen to spend the day with us, off-duty. Her care and concern for us eased a bit of the emptiness left by my parents' absence. Not only did I respect her as a professional, but she'd grown into a part of our family unit.

"Hank thinks it's a good idea," Tuck said.

I gave him a questioning sideways glance. "Are you telepathic or what?"

"No." He smirked. The sight of his dimples sent a thunderbolt of sexual awareness straight between my thighs. "Hank has a lot to say. Don't you, bud?" Tuck turned the brim of his baseball cap to the rear and leaned forward to rest his forearms on the back of the chair. "For instance, right now, he's saying, 'I hate having my hair cut but I'll tolerate it because it makes you happy.'"

"Oh, really?" I tried not to laugh but noticed the way Hank's mouth twitched.

"And he also says that he hates his shirt. It's pink, and only girls wear pink."

"It's not pink. It's salmon." I placed a hand on Hank's shoulder and bent to look into his eyes. "You don't like this shirt? Seriously?" Hank blinked twice, confirming Tuck's insight. I turned to Tucker, hands on my hips. "What else does Hank have to say?"

Tuck shrugged. "A whole lot more, but it's mostly guy stuff and I really can't tell you." He winked at him. The sparkle in Hank's eyes brought a lump to my throat. "Right, Hank?"

My brother grunted.

"Fine." I shook my head, warmed by their exchange. "Alright. I'll think about it."

Tuck stayed in the living room while I returned the scissors and comb to the small bathroom next to the kitchen. Hillary was waiting for me when I came out.

"It's a lot of work," I said to her, lowering my voice.

"Look at them." She gestured toward the living room.

Tuck had pulled his chair closer to Hank's bed and was carrying on an in-depth one-sided conversation. Hank watched him, eyes bright, nodding his head. It was the most animated I'd ever seen him. Observing them, it made my chest ache, but in a good way. Tuck brought a lightness to our household that had been missing for years, since our parents had died.

"Do this for Hank," Hillary said. I shook my head and tried to walk away, but she caught me by the arm. "It's okay to let people in. Take a risk. You can't protect him all the time."

No, I couldn't, but I could try. I could bear my own pain, but I couldn't bear his. I pulled my arm away.

"Not everyone is like Cody," she said. The sound of my ex-boyfriend's name brought with it the familiar, sharp stab of regret.

"It has nothing to do with Cody," I said, but it was a lie. My breakup with Cody had shaped the way I dealt with men, my attitudes toward relationships, and my inability to trust anyone. He'd walked away from me when I'd needed him most, left me when I was vulnerable and hurting. I couldn't risk letting that happen again.

"Don't make Hank suffer because of your fears." Hillary rested a hand on my shoulder and squeezed.

From the living room, Tuck continued to talk with Hank. The last thing I wanted to do was punish my brother for circumstances beyond his control. He'd already paid a tremendous price. I'd move heaven and earth to see him smile, to bring even one minute of happiness into his pitiful life. Giving him this small gift was the least I could do.

"Okay." I exhaled, ruffling the bangs over my forehead. "Can I talk to you for a minute? Over here?" I didn't want my brother to hear our exchange.

"You won't have to do a thing," Tuck said, as if reading my thoughts. "I'll take care of all the details." He patted Hank on the shoulder. "I'll be back in a sec, bro."

At the edge of the hallway, I tugged him aside. "Are you sure about this? I mean, do you understand how big a deal this is for him?"

Tucker stared down at me in the dim light. His body heat permeated the narrow space between us. I tried to ignore the sweet, woodsy scent of his aftershave. The span of his broad chest lifted and fell with each of his breaths. My breasts ached, the nipples teased into tight buds at his proximity. Less than four inches separated our bodies. It took all of my willpower to avoid melting against him.

"Don't worry. I won't fuck it up." The square line of his jaw sharpened. I tilted my chin to take in the full beauty of his lips, the straight nose, the stubble on his cheeks.

"It's hard for me to trust people. I've been let down. Hank's been let down—a lot. Don't be one of those people." I had no idea how to explain the disaster of my relationship with Cody, or Hank's heartbreak over Neve. Everyone I'd ever cared about left or disappointed me. My parents had left against their will. Cody had walked away willingly. In my mind, both incidents held equal weight. I wanted to believe in Tucker. I wanted to trust him. I just didn't know how.

By the time the next Saturday arrived, I'd managed to work myself into a state of panic. My stomach ached and my palms were slick with sweat. Tucker arrived an hour early with his brother Tate and Tyler, Caleb, and the caterer. They set up a mountain of food on the kitchen table. Ten minutes after their appearance, Hillary answered a second knock on the door, and I had to wonder how many people he'd actually invited. The thought of strangers in my house made me uneasy. I'd managed to create a safe environment for Hank, one where he could exist without risk to his mental or physical wellbeing. The introduction of unknown elements threatened the delicate balance of our household and created a knot in the pit of my belly.

"I'm Abraham Wells, ma'am. Nice to meet you." The greeting came from a towering man with soft brown eyes and a smooth, comforting voice. He shook Hillary's hand then mine in a firm grip with fingers the size of sausages. "I'm supposed to ask for Tucker Spaulding."

"Abe. Good to see you." Tucker appeared at my side and clapped Abe on the back. "Abe's a private duty nurse and a friend of my sister's. He's offered to come and work with Hank today so you and Hillary can enjoy the game."

"Oh, okay." I blinked then tugged Tucker to the side. "I appreciate the thought behind this, but I don't know this guy."

Tucker stared back at me, a stubborn set to his lips. "My sister's a nurse, and she's known him for years. A lot longer than you've known those losers from the agency. He's the best. He specializes in care for people like Hank. I can get his references if it makes you feel better."

Hillary joined our conversation while Abe talked to Hank. The empathy in his deep voice as he spoke to my brother told me more about his character than any words of recommendation. I sighed and looked away, refusing to meet the gazes of Tuck and Hillary. I'd been Hank's sole caretaker for so long that I had no idea how to relinquish the slightest bit of control. The idea of relaxing my hold sent my senses into a tailspin.

"I said you could have a few friends here. I didn't say you could take over our lives," I snapped. "Hank's my responsibility. You've got no right to make choices for him without my consent."

"Okay," Tuck said, bewilderment obvious in his tone. He lifted his palms into the air. "I can send him home if you like. I just thought you might appreciate a little help from someone you can trust."

Hillary lowered her eyebrows in her motherly, you're-fucking-up-again kind of way.

I pressed a hand to my stomach and tried to ease the tightness there. "Fine. It's fine. I just need a minute." I fled to the upstairs bathroom and shut the door behind me. I sat on the edge of the bathtub and focused on my breathing. Everything was fine. This wasn't a big deal. I had nothing to worry about. And I had to get over my stupid need to control every little detail. For Hank.

From the bathroom window, I peered at the cars in the driveway. A classic Corvette, some kind of Bentley, and a BMW i8 lined the street. Tucker had some fancy friends, and the thought of meeting them made my knees weak. I didn't do well with strangers or people in general. I watched them parade up the sidewalk, laughing and smiling. They looked fun, nice, and carefree—all the things I wanted to be but wasn't. Not anymore. And it had been so long since I was those things, I wasn't sure I remembered how to be anything other than a recluse.

A knock vibrated the door. "Fallon? Can I come in?" Tuck's voice quickened the beat of my heart. So there was *that* issue as well. Every time he touched me or bent to speak in my ear, my body did some crazy things. I didn't have the time or the energy to deal with romantic feelings. Hank deserved my full and undivided attention and there was no room for a guy in it, not even one as great as Tucker.

"No. I mean, yes." I caught a glimpse of my reflection in the mirror over the sink and smoothed my hair. Somber eyes stared back at me. When had they become so sad? Compared to Tucker's friends, I appeared uptight and older than my twenty-three years.

He opened the door, stepped inside the bathroom, then shut the door behind him, trapping me in the small space with his maleness, his muscles, and the clean scent that was uniquely his. I closed my eyes, unwilling to look at him after my mini-tantrum.

"What's the deal?" he asked with a good deal more patience than I deserved. "If you want us to go, we'll go. I just thought it would be good for Hank and for you to meet some new people, different people."

I huffed out a sigh and brushed my palms over the tops of my denim-clad thighs. "I know. You're right. It's fine. I just—" I had no idea how to articulate the tangle of conflicting thoughts in my head, so I stared at the tips of my toes peeking from the ends of my sandals.

"Why can't you talk to me?" The amount of frustration in his tone caught me by surprise. I glanced up in time to see him run a hand through his hair.

"I don't know. It's me. I'm fucked up. Don't worry about it." Intending to leave, I stood up, but he blocked my escape with his broad shoulders. When his palm rested on the small of my back, fingers spread wide, a shudder of need rippled through my body. I looked into his face and found his eyes searching mine with an intensity too blatant to be ignored. My ribs ached from the rapid-fire beat of my heart.

"Everyone's fucked up in one way or another, Fallon," he said.

We were chest to chest. The tips of my breasts rubbed against the thin fabric of his T-shirt. My nipples tightened, against my will, into hard nubs. With every rise and fall of his ribs, the friction increased the sensation, sending tiny jolts of electricity into my legs, my fingers, and the space between my legs.

Oh, God. He was going to kiss me. I saw the warning flash of hunger in his eyes, the way they locked onto my mouth. His tongue slid over his lower lip, and his soft breath puffed against my mouth. Blood raced through my veins.

He pulled me closer with one hand on my back and pressed his open lips to mine.

It had been so long since anyone had kissed me. I'd forgotten the sensation of being held by a man, how large his hands were, the hardness of his muscles, and how utterly female it made me feel. His heartbeat pulsed against my breast. His fingers curled against my back then slid down to grip my hip. I opened my mouth, let my tongue slide against his, inhaled his breath, and lost myself.

His lips widened, sealing over mine, crushing against me. The sweet, sharp bite of his peppermint candy sizzled on my tongue. A bevy of sensations collided and sent my head spinning. I leaned into him, molding my body to his. His cock hardened between us and pushed against the waist of my shorts. My hands crept up his chest. I clenched my fingers in the fabric of his T-shirt and clung to him.

"Tucker? Tuck!" Caleb called his name from the other side of the door, feet from where we stood.

Tucker pushed away. His lips were red, face flushed. Both of us struggled for breath, like we'd been running a footrace. A tidal wave of embarrassment heated my neck and cheeks. Had I gone too far? Oh God, had I moaned out loud? Yes, I had. I was sure of it. I uncurled my fingers from his T-shirt and smoothed out the dents in the fabric.

"We'd better get out there," he said in a raw voice, his words stilted.

His chest heaved beneath my palms. I was still touching him. "Yes." My voice broke on the single syllable. "Yes. You go ahead. I'll be out in a second."

I needed a minute alone to straighten my clothes and get a grip on my tempestuous hormones. My hands shook as I ran a brush through my hair. What was I doing? I didn't want to get involved with anyone ever again—even someone as kind and generous as Tucker. He wasn't interested in me. Or was he? I stared at my reflection in the mirror. My eyes shone, the pink of my lips heightened by Tucker's mouth against mine. I hadn't imagined his passion. I pressed a finger to my mouth, reliving the fire in his kiss, and dared to dream for one heartbeat that he felt the same way about me.

The roar of voices and laughter filled the house. Aromas of fried chicken and hot wings scented the air. Back when my parents were alive, they'd had friends over on the weekends and barbecued in the back yard. Sounds and smells of the party reminded me how much I missed the company of other people.

The room overflowed with guests. I sat on a chair near the foyer, feeling like an outsider in my own home. Les and Hillary sat together on the loveseat. Les curled an arm around her shoulders. His fingers toyed with the ends of her short hair, lighting her face with smiles. Venetia and Piers Beckett took up residence in one of the recliners. They'd brought their three-month-old baby, an adorable little girl with a pert nose and white-blond hair. She rested on her father's lap, thumb in her mouth, eyes closed, asleep amid the noise. Tucker's younger brother, Tyler, stood next to Hank's bed and chatted with him about scores and stats. He looked to be about the same age, dressed in cargo shorts and a muscle shirt. He was a darker version of Tucker, clean-cut and polite, but wore the same lazy smile. Caleb, and Tucker's "mechanic" Roni, sat on the floor near the TV, eyes glued to the game while Tate clapped his hands and shouted insults at the umpires. Everyone wore smiles, conversation flowed easily around the room, and Hank looked happy.

"Fallon, do you mind if I use your restroom?" Venetia asked. As she spoke, she moved from the arm of the recliner and tucked a silky strand of her long, blond hair behind her ear. Of all the guests, she appeared to be the closest to my age, but we had little else in common. She was tall, willowy, and reeked of wealth, whereas I was shorter, boyish, and one step away from the poorhouse. The bracelet on her wrist had probably cost more than my entire salary. Next to her tailored white shorts and striped sailor shirt, my cut-off jeans and T-shirt seemed ratty.

I tugged the hem of my tee self-consciously. "Sure. Not at all." I stood and led her to the hallway. "It's down there. Second door to the left."

"Your house is really cute." As she spoke, her gaze wandered along the crown moldings, the transoms over the doors, and the hardwood floors. "If you ever want to modify the inside for Hank, I'd be happy to help." She pressed a business card into my hand. "I run an interior design company, and I've had some experience in customizing homes for people with special needs. I'm doing the renovations on Tuck's office right now. You can ask him about the quality of my work."

"Thanks." I took the card and turned it over in my fingers, unsure how to comment. "I know it needs help, but I don't really have the money." I didn't want her pity, but the house did need work.

"You know, there are lots of organizations out there who'd love to help you. I could put you in touch with people, if you wanted."

"That's very nice of you." I bit my lower lip, embarrassed by her kindness. "I've tried before, and didn't have much success."

"Well, you didn't have me on your side," she said with a

deep-dimpled smile so disarming, I found myself smiling back at her. "It's the least I can do, considering what you've done for Tucker." I searched her face, certain she was joking, but found only sincerity in her blue eyes.

"You're welcome." The response came automatically out of my mouth because I had no idea what she meant.

"He's been so down since—well, since Sydney—since the wedding, you know?"

A sickening ball rolled around my stomach. He had said it was a bad breakup. Was Tucker divorced or had he been engaged? I didn't like thinking of him with another woman, even though I had no claim to him.

"I think being around you, it's really helped him get his mind off things." She touched my forearm and smiled. Tucker shared very little about himself, and I was starved to know more. I hadn't gotten up the nerve to search the internet again, afraid I'd see him with another girl.

"He's the one who saved us," I replied. My gaze drifted to the living room, where Tuck sat beside Hank, chatting to him about the last play. My brother watched him with shining eyes and a bloom of color on his cheeks. I swallowed back a lump of emotion in my throat. "What happened with Sydney?"

"Oh, he hasn't told you?" Venetia paled as if she realized her mistake. "I assumed you knew. He said—well, he said you were close." Warmth filled my chest to know he'd spoken about me to someone else, someone in his inner circle of friends. "It's not my place to tell, but you should ask him."

Apparently the game had taken a turn for the worst, and a shout rang out from the living room. My lips still burned with Tuck's kiss while my mind stung from the way he'd shut down immediately after. It all made sense now; his sad eyes, why he rarely smiled. His heart was broken.

The doorbell rang, and I excused myself to greet the next arrival. I opened the door to find a tall man on the steps. Sunlight glinted off his blond head. He extended a bottle of wine, expensive by the look of the label, and offered his hand.

"Hi. You must be Fallon. I'm Samuel Seaforth," he said, in a rich, commanding voice. "It's a pleasure to meet you."

My mouth dropped open. Samuel Seaforth, business powerhouse, stood on my front porch wearing navy blue Bermuda shorts and a pristine white polo shirt, looking like he'd just come from the country club. Shoot, he probably *had* just come from the country club, the one I'd never been to but had driven past a thousand times during my life. I gaped at him, star struck.

"Don't be impressed." Tucker's lips brushed my earlobe, and his deep voice reverberated through my auditory canal, straight down to my toes. He leaned over my shoulder. "I have it on good authority that he was a bed-wetter until he was twenty."

"Really? Talking smack about me already?" Sam arched an eyebrow at Tucker then his lips curled in a blinding grin. "You can't believe a thing he says, Fallon. He's ninety percent bullshit, ten percent crap."

"It's nice—good—great to meet you," I stammered and took his hand, aware of Tucker's chest against my backside. The touch of his body against mine caused a pleasant tightening deep inside my tummy.

"A pleasure to meet you as well. My wife sends her regrets. She's been under the weather lately." Sam shoved the wine bottle at Tucker and engulfed both of my hands in his. They exchanged a look, one I couldn't decipher, but I had the feeling an entire conversation had passed between them.

"Hey, big brother. Is Dakota okay?" Venetia returned from the bathroom. She stood on tiptoe to give Sam a kiss on the cheek. I hadn't realized Venetia was a Seaforth as well. Two Seaforths in my crappy little house? I made a mental note to catalog this day in my journal, because no one would ever believe me later.

"She's...doing as well as can be expected, I guess." Although I didn't know Sam, his voice carried a palpable undercurrent of anxiety.

"Is there anything I can do?" Venetia asked. Her worried eyes searched her brother's face.

"No. She just needs time," he said. They might be aristocrats, but apparently they suffered their problems like everyone else.

A little of my anxiety eased to learn I wasn't the only person with challenges. "Please, come on in. Make yourself at home." I took the bottle of wine from Tucker and set it on the table near the door. We made our way into the living room as another shout went up from the spectators. I crowded onto the sofa between Sam and Tucker. He stretched an arm behind my shoulders. The gesture seemed casual enough, but excitement skated along my nerve endings every time his chest brushed my arm or his thigh pressed against mine.

"You owe me five hundred bucks, Tucker," Beckett, Venetia's fiancé, growled. He had left his seat to stand near the TV, the sleeping baby balanced on one arm, the top of his black head nearly brushing the seven-foot ceiling. I'd never heard of Venetia, but I knew of Piers Beckett, had seen his face on television. He'd handled some of the most scathing celebrity divorces in the country. Right now, he looked like any other baseball fan, dressed in a Red's jersey and cap.

"Game's not over yet, Shorty," Tucker replied. Goosebumps crawled over my arms at the sound of his lazy twang. When had that happened? When had the mere sound of his voice sent my hormones into a tailspin? He turned to Hank. "What do you think, Hank? Should we go double or nothing?"

Hank nodded, a grin of pure delight on his face, and I forgot to care about Tuck's financial status or the way his kiss had set my lips on fire. The sight of Hank's relaxed, easy demeanor caught the breath in my lungs, and I placed a hand on my chest. He looked almost normal, almost happy, the way he had before the accident. And I owed it all to Tuck.

While the game continued, Tuck's fingers brushed the back of my neck, making it hard to concentrate on anything but him. The tiny hairs on my nape stood erect, my skin sizzled, and my breasts ached to be touched. Feelings of lust had become so much more, and the intensity of my emotions continued to swell. I was falling in love with him.

After everyone had gone, Tucker stayed to clean up. We washed dishes together while Les picked up the living room. Abe prepared Hank for bed under the watchful eye of Hillary. I had to admit, Abe seemed more than capable, and Hank appeared to like him. The poor guy was exhausted by all the excitement and was asleep by the time Tucker went to leave.

I walked him to the front steps. "This was good," I said, ducking my head. Expressing my feelings had never been easy, especially when they were so overwhelming. I was afraid to show how much his kiss affected me in case he didn't feel the same. "For Hank, I mean. I haven't seen him happy like that since—in a long time."

"My pleasure," Tucker replied. We stood toe to toe, not touching, but I could feel him in every part of my body, every nerve ending humming at his proximity. "He's a good kid. I like helping him."

"Your friends are nice. You didn't tell me you hang out with celebrities." I kept my tone light, but my fingers curled with the need to touch him.

"They've always been there for me. They're good people to have in your corner." He lifted a hand and stroked along the hollow of my cheek

My pulse beat a rapid tattoo in the curve of my neck. "I get the feeling you're a good person to have in my corner too," I replied, and before I could overthink it, I turned my face and dropped a kiss into his palm. His hand slipped to the back of my head, fingers digging into my nape. Our mouths snapped together in a hot, wet kiss. I fell back against the house. The wood siding bit into my back as he pressed me into the wall. Desire clenched all the muscles below my waist.

I gripped his back, feeling the ripple of muscle along his spine as he took my mouth, hard and possessive. One of his knees split my thighs. His free hand found my bottom and squeezed. The blatant outline of his erection nudged my tummy. For the first time in years, I allowed myself to want —make that *need*—more. My fingers tangled in his hair as our mouths grew more frantic.

"Wait." The tortured emotion in Tuck's voice cleared the fog of pleasure in my brain. He reared back, bracing an arm on the side of the house above my shoulder. "I can't."

A wave of crushing rejection bowled over me. For the

second time that day, he was pushing me away. I dropped my hands to my side, feeling the sting of humiliation in the form of tears. Cody had pushed me away, said I was too clinging, too needy. I didn't want to drive Tucker away also.

"It's not you," he said, his words textured and thick. He took a step back, and cool air filtered into the space between us. I shivered and wrapped my arms around my chest to hide the tight peaks of my nipples. "You said you're fucked up. Well, I'm fucked up, too. A lot. And I don't want to hurt you. You—Hank—you both mean too much to me."

"Is it because of Sydney?" I asked.

He looked away, into the darkness, staring at a place far beyond my sight. His shoulders lifted and dropped with a sigh. "What do you know about Sydney?"

The amount of anger in his voice confused me. Apparently, I'd touched on a tender subject. I stammered. "Nothing. I just— Venetia said—well, you never said what happened with her. I just thought—"

"I don't want to talk about Syd. Not ever." He shoved a hand through his hair. "Look, it's been a long day. You should get some rest, so I'm going to go. I'll talk to you later."

Before I could recover my wits, he was down the sidewalk and climbing into the BMW. The car zoomed down the street and disappeared around the corner, leaving me on the porch, breathing hard and feeling like I'd been run over by a truck.

14

TUCKER

Later that night, as I lay awake in bed, no matter how hard I tried, I failed to conjure up Sydney's face. Instead, Fallon's amber eyes and pink lips floated in my head. Crushing guilt burned through my veins. I still felt Fallon's soft mouth on mine, the press of her breasts against my chest. The scent of her perfume lingered on my clothes, her taste on my tongue. If my love for Sydney was true, how could I have such intense feelings for Fallon? I believed in love and fidelity. In my experience, it wasn't possible to love two women at the same time, not without being unfaithful to one of them. I didn't want to be that guy, the one who used one woman to get over another. I liked and respected Fallon too much to be so callous.

Desperate and confused, I pulled up Sydney's picture on my phone. It was the last photo I'd taken of her, a quick selfie of the two of us on the sidewalk outside her hotel. She was laughing, head thrown back, wind whipping her black hair across her face. Seeing her brought back the ice pick of pain in my chest, the deep ache of her loss still present but dulled by the passage of time. As I stared at her picture, I saw the face of a stranger, not the woman I'd loved. The woman I loved didn't exist. She'd been a figment of my imagination, a carefully crafted character played out by a skilled actor.

On Monday, I purposely avoided the train and drove to work instead. Tuesday, I stayed late at the office, working into the early hours on the latest game, trying to exhaust myself. I spent the night on the sofa in the Inner Sanctum. When my eyes finally closed of their own accord, Fallon haunted my dreams and not Sydney.

The buzz of my phone woke me Wednesday morning. I answered, disoriented, without looking to identify the caller, and heard Sam's commanding voice.

"You're late," he said, a bit of amusement lacing his words. "You owe us each twenty bucks."

"Shit." I rolled onto my feet. "Be there in ten."

Every Wednesday, I met up with Sam and Beckett. Sometimes we played basketball; other times we had breakfast before work or drinks after. Today, we were meeting for breakfast at the bistro down the street. By the time I arrived, both men were seated at a table on the open-air patio, sharp in their three-piece suits.

"You look like shit." Beckett ran a skeptical gaze up and down my rumpled T-shirt and jeans, the same clothes I'd slept in.

"Thanks." I pulled a chair alongside the table and slapped two twenty-dollar bills on their placemats, the penalty for tardiness to one of our outings. "I haven't been sleeping much."

"Work or personal?" Sam arched an eyebrow.

"Both, I guess. I've got a new game in the works."

The waitress stopped in front of me and smiled as she

placed a glass of water on the table. Our conversation halted. "The usual?" she asked.

"Yes, please," I replied.

"How's Hank doing?" Beckett asked as soon as the waitress moved to the next customer.

"I don't know. I haven't been there this week. Too busy." To hide my conflicted feelings, I took a swallow from my water glass. Both men regarded me, their stares relentless.

"Seems like a cool kid. Shame to see him laid up like that. Can we help them out?" Sam took his napkin from the table and snapped it in the air before placing it on his lap.

"Venetia's already on it," Beckett added. "She started texting her contacts before we pulled out of Fallon's driveway Saturday. You know how she eats that shit up." His deep voice held a note of pride. The way her eyes lit when she saw him, his smile for her, their beautiful baby— these were all things I imagined for myself someday, or had. My hopes had been dashed when Sydney had left.

"Have you guys set a date yet?" I asked, hoping to steer the conversation away from Fallon. Each time someone spoke her name, my pulse leaped. I tugged at the collar of my shirt.

"Good question. When are you going to make an honest woman out of my sister?" Sam leveled his intimidating gaze on Beckett. "Or do you plan to shack up for the rest of your lives?" In spite of his menacing tone, Sam was thrilled to have Beckett as a brother-in-law, and I envied their connection. They were both committed to loving, beautiful women. By contrast, my romantic history consisted of a string of one-nighters with random girls from the bar, and being dumped by a B-list actress.

"Talk to V." Beckett's narrowed his eyes. "I've been trying, but the girl does what she wants on her own schedule. You know how she is." His sigh spoke volumes about his frustration. "She said she wants to lose the baby weight first."

"A Christmas wedding would be nice," I said, prolonging Beckett's discomfort for the fun of it. Before the breakup, he'd teased me mercilessly about Sydney. I wasn't going to let him off the hook without a little payback. "You could fly everyone out to Jamaica or St. Thomas and do it on the beach."

Beckett smoothed a hand over his blue tie and glared at me. "And who's going to pay for that? Unlike you, I'm not made of money."

"We all know you're sitting on fat pile of cash," I said. "Or let V pay for it." I smiled, knowing I'd touched a nerve. Beckett was too traditional to let his bride foot the bill for her own wedding.

"Like hell." His eyes flashed. Sam pressed his lips together to stifle a smile. I bit the inside of my cheek to hold back my own grin. "That money is for her and for our baby. She's going to have her dream wedding, and I'm not going to make her pay for it. What kind of a schmuck do you think I am?"

Sam and I burst out laughing.

A red flush crept up Beckett's neck as he realized our game. He shook his head and smiled. "You're an ass. Both of you."

"You fall for it every time. I couldn't help myself." I relaxed a little, easing into the familiar safety of our friendship.

"Speaking of falling..." Beckett adjusted his chair to face me. "Fallon's a pretty girl, don't you think?"

Heat rushed into my face. I cleared my throat and leaned away from the table as the waitress placed a plate of pancakes in front of me. Beckett and Sam exchanged a glance but remained quiet until the waitress left. A pigeon milled at our feet, pecking morsels of dropped food. I stared at it, grateful to have somewhere to gaze besides at my friends. One look at my face and they'd be able to see my conflict.

"You asked her out yet?" Sam spoke first as he stirred a spoonful of brown sugar into a bowl of oatmeal.

"Not exactly." I turned my attention on slathering butter over my pancakes then drizzling warm blueberry syrup over the top. "Just for coffee. She turned me down."

"That's not a date," Sam said.

"Why not?" Beckett stared at me over the top of a plate heaped with hash browns and eggs.

"Why would I?" I shoveled a forkful of food into my mouth. The fluffy pancake melted on my tongue, and I hummed in appreciation.

"Well, she's pretty and smart," Sam said.

"And sweet and into you," Beckett added.

"She's not into me." Even as I spoke the words, their meaning sparked hope in my chest. Did I want her to be interested in me? I swallowed and washed down the food with a drink of water. I'd been too absorbed in Hank and denying my attraction to Fallon to ever consider that it might be a two-way street.

"Oh man, you're so wrong." The legs of Beckett's chair scraped across the patio as he pushed back from the table. The noise sent the pigeon thundering into flight. In typical Beckett fashion, he'd inhaled his food and finished in record time. "I was there. I saw how she looked at you. She's hot for you."

I shook my head and stared at my plate. "You're just saying that because you're hooked up with V and Sam's got Dakota. You can't stand it that I'm single and you're not."

Sam snorted. He tossed his napkin onto the table and leaned toward me. "Not true. But you haven't dated anyone at all since Syd. Time to move on, don't you think?"

"Yeah, we're tired of your sorry single ass at our dinner parties," Beckett added.

I knew he was teasing, but his words touched a sore spot. For the past few months, I'd been the odd man, watching from the outside as my best friends embarked on a path down which I couldn't follow. Once we'd done everything together—first as college friends then later as adults. I missed hitting the bars and hanging out on the weekends. Now, they were both in committed relationships while I had no one. "I'm not looking for a relationship."

"A date is not a relationship," Beckett said. As he spoke, he thumbed through a stack of bills in his wallet then tossed a few singles onto the table.

"You need to get back on the horse." Sam flashed his black credit card at the waitress as she passed, signaling for the check. "Time to move on. Sydney did."

"I don't give a rat's ass about Sydney." My words were too sharp and bitter to be convincing.

Really?" Beckett lifted an eyebrow. "That's good, because she's back."

She's back. Those two words sent my morning into a tailspin.

I left breakfast feeling unsettled and numb. Sydney was back. Back in town. *Back.* I scanned the face of each person I passed along the street, wondering if it might be her. My heart leaped at the sight of a black-haired girl at the crosswalk then plummeted to find it was someone else. I couldn't spend the next few weeks wondering when I might run into her, where she was, or what she was doing. Why did I even care? She didn't care about me. She'd left me for another man, had been using me the entire time, fooling me into thinking she loved me when she didn't. The more I thought about it, the angrier I became. I wanted to punch someone, break something, anything to release a little of the rage inside me.

By the time I reached Twisted Wire Productions, my thoughts were an incoherent, jumbled mess. I needed to get away, to clear my head. I sent Caleb a text message and asked him to join me in the Inner Sanctum for an emergency meeting.

"What?" Caleb burst into the room. "Where's the fire?"

"Venezuela. We're leaving as soon as I can get a flight out." I already had the permit to make the jump at Angel Falls. Since meeting Fallon and Hank, I'd put the adventure aside, but now it seemed like a matter of utmost urgency. I needed the rush, the thrill of cheating death. Most of all, I needed the clarity provided from a good jump.

"No." By the irritation in his voice, he was fully awake now. "After what you did last time? Hell if I'm going to participate in another one of your suicide missions."

I scrubbed a hand over my face, irrational anger tugged on my temper. "Fine. Don't go then." Caleb had been my wingman since I'd started jumping. Although it felt wrong to go without him, I didn't need him or his permission. I started to hang up, but his response stopped me.

"Dude, I thought maybe you were over this—this obsession of yours. What about Hank? And Fallon?"

"They'll be fine." A different kind of guilt assuaged me. I pushed it aside. I didn't want to think about Fallon, or my uncontrollable urge to take care of her. "Tell them I'll see them when I get back."

Caleb's deep inhale was audible over the phone. "You're an idiot, throwing away something good over a girl who doesn't give two shits about you."

His words wounded me in a way I hadn't known possible. "Screw you." I started to hang up.

"No. Screw you. I know you don't want to admit this, but you and Sydney were never a thing. You were fuck buddies. And somewhere along the line, you forgot that."

I disconnected the call before he could say more. Truth rang in his admonition. My relationship with Sydney had always been one-sided. She'd never said she loved me, never asked for more than sex, never encouraged my affections beyond the physical. I threw my phone against the wall and watched it shatter into a hundred pieces, like my heart.

15

———

FALLON

Tucker didn't show up on Tuesday evening. I resisted the urge to call or text him. His vacillating behavior suggested he was in a fragile state. I didn't want to embarrass myself by chasing after him or jeopardize our friendship by pushing him into something he didn't want. When I didn't hear from him for the rest of the week, my old insecurities reared their heads to taunt and undermine my confidence. Maybe Tucker was embarrassed about our kiss. Maybe he didn't want to hurt my feelings. I missed his company more than I cared to admit. My life centered around Hank and his needs; time with Tucker was the only respite I got, the only time for myself. After putting Hank first for so long, I was beginning to lose my identity, to forget who I was and what I wanted from life. Tucker gave me a taste of what I was missing.

The weekdays blurred into one. On Saturday, I rolled out of bed early, determined to make the most of my day. Abe had agreed to take care of Hank on the weekends at a surprisingly reasonable rate. I suspected Tucker had had a hand in Abe's discount fees, but Abe denied it. Knowing

Hank was in Abe's capable hands eased a ton of weight off my shoulders and provided me with the freedom to run errands and breathe for the first time. I took a few precious hours for myself and splurged on a new haircut, highlights, and a manicure.

When I arrived home, my heart danced at the sight of the pickup truck parked in front of the house. Caleb pushed the mower along the hedge and stopped to greet me. He dragged a forearm across his forehead to wipe away beads of perspiration. Heat shimmered over the pavement of the driveway.

"Hey, Caleb. Is Tucker inside?" I asked, eager to get his take on my new look.

"No. He couldn't make it," he replied.

"Oh." Bitter disappointment tempered my former enthusiasm. "Okay." I started toward the house then stopped. "Did I do something? I mean, is he mad at me? I haven't heard from him all week." I brushed the hair back from my forehead. "I'm sorry. I shouldn't be asking you."

Caleb studied me for a long moment, as if weighing what and how much he should divulge. "He's in Venezuela, making a jump."

My mouth went dry. Somehow, I'd conveniently chosen to forget Tucker's reckless streak in the face of his generosity and friendship. Now, it came rushing back with the force of an atomic bomb. "Where?" I managed to ask.

"Angel Falls." Sensing my horror, Caleb's brown eyes softened. He rubbed my shoulder. "Don't worry, he's jumped hundreds of times. I'm sure he'll be fine. The stupid ass," he added under his breath.

"Why does he do it? Is he crazy?" Fear weakened my knees and made the world spin. I sank to the porch steps and tried to recover my composure.

"He's a black death jumper," Caleb said. "Do you know what that means?"

I shook my head and placed a hand on my chest to soothe the ache of my racing heart. "No, but I don't like the sound of it."

"It means he jumps to confront death. He says it makes him feel more alive, but I'm not so sure anymore." The sober gravity in his eyes did little to comfort my unease. "It's one thing to jump for the fun of it. It's another to do it for emotional reasons."

A million unpleasant thoughts whirled through my head. What if he got hurt? So many things could go wrong. His parachute could fail. He might slip and hit his head like Hank had done. Life changed in the blink of an eye, often in unexpected and unpleasant ways. No one knew it better than I did. "Why would he do something like that?" I whispered.

"Ever since Sydney, he's had this wild thing inside him. It's like he's taunting fate. You and Hank distracted him for a while, but..." His voice trailed off, and he shrugged. "I probably should have gone with him. I just couldn't stand by and watch him take chances like that again. I thought if I stayed here, he might change his mind."

"This Sydney—who is she? I asked him the other day, and he wouldn't tell me." Just speaking this person's name made my stomach churn, like I was betraying Tucker's trust, but I needed to know.

"Sydney Marcus." Caleb waited for me to make the connection then nodded as my eyes widened. "Yeah, that's the one."

I knew the girl—or at least knew of her. Everyone did. Her wedding to the co-star of her TV series had made reality show history and instigated a media shit storm. A vision of a vibrant, black-haired girl with a bright smile and sparkling eyes crossed my memories. Silly me, I'd assumed Sydney was an average person. Not only did I feel crushing sympathy for Tucker, I also felt like a fool for thinking he was interested in someone as plain and unexciting as me.

"I thought she had a boyfriend on the show." I furrowed my brow, trying to remember the details.

"Yeah, she did, but she was stringing Tuck along on the side. And Tuck took it hard when she got married." Caleb nodded, as if confirming his own internal suspicions. "He's not been the same since."

Now I got it. The way he ran hot and cold. The guarded look in his eyes. Hurt and disappointment rolled around inside me. I was such an idiot, letting my emotions ran rampant, thinking he might have feelings for me. He couldn't care for me, because he already cared for someone else. The best I could hope for was to be his rebound, and everyone knew rebounds didn't last.

"You really like him, don't you?" He smiled and rubbed my shoulder, but the sadness remained in his eyes. "Look. Don't worry. He'll be fine. He's got a crew of professionals with him." Almost as an afterthought, he added, "And don't tell him I said anything about Sydney, would you? He'll be really pissed about it."

"Sure. My lips are sealed." I gave him a smile, but on the inside I wanted to cry. "Well, I need to get back inside. Thanks for everything." I gathered up my strength and headed into the house, where Abe and Caleb were watching a baseball game. Abe nodded as I entered the room. "I'll be upstairs if you need me," I said. "I've got a headache. I'm going to lie down for a bit."

"We're good down here," Abe said. "Take your time."

Instead of going to my room, I went into my parents'

bedroom and closed the door behind me. Even after three years, I still couldn't bring myself to clear out their things. I opened the closet, took out my mother's fuzzy bathrobe, and lifted it to my nose. The scent of her perfume still lingered. I climbed into the robe and curled up on the bed. If I closed my eyes, the warm robe *almost* felt like her arms around me.

Tears oozed from the corners of my eyes, but I wiped them away. I hadn't cried over a boy since Cody, and I wasn't going to start now. My heart hurt for Tucker, but I had no idea how to heal him when I couldn't heal myself.

The following Saturday, Tucker arrived in the morning with Caleb, acting like nothing had happened, like he hadn't been gone for two weeks. *You can do this, Fallon. Be cool. Be grateful for his friendship.* What choice did I have? I mean, he'd been involved with a television celebrity, one of the most beautiful girls in Hollywood. Why would he ever look at a geek like me? On the other hand, he'd kissed me twice, hard and hot and wet. I'd been kissed enough to know the difference between a friendly peck and a sexual claiming. It had to mean something. This was exactly the reason I hadn't wanted him coming around in the first place. He'd made me care and then he'd disappeared, just like my parents, just like Cody.

My parents had no choice in the matter. Their lives had ended when a drunk driver had crossed the centerline and collided into their car. I accepted the situation for what it was—an accident. Cody was a different matter. We'd been friends since elementary school, dated through senior year of high school and beyond. After Hank had come home from the hospital, Cody had visited us once and then he'd never visited again. No excuses, no phone calls, nothing but silence.

With Tucker, I could understand if he didn't want to see me. Maybe we'd taken things too far that night. What I couldn't forgive was the way he'd left Hank high and dry. He had so little light in his life, and Tucker had taken it away. Knowing these things didn't stop me from remembering the way he'd kissed me, the way his hands had felt on my ass, or the way he'd groaned into my mouth.

Unable to stand the confusion and frustration of my feelings, I asked Abe to watch over Hank for a few minutes while I walked to the convenience store. I didn't really have a reason to leave, but I needed the fresh air and a few minutes to think. Maybe Tuck would be gone by the time I returned.

No such luck. When I got back, I found him standing in the living room, chatting to Hank. My heart thudded so hard against my ribs, I thought they might crack. He was shirtless, jeans hanging low on his hips. An oh-so-hot trail of hair led from his navel into the waistband of his pants. I swallowed hard and forced my gaze up to his face.

"Hey," he said. He rubbed his palms on his jeans and shifted from one foot to the other.

"Hello." I frowned and glanced around, anything to avoid his gaze. "Where's Abe?"

"He ran out for a minute. I told him I'd stay with Hank until he got back." He licked his lips, centering my attention on his mouth. The tender flesh between my legs began to ache at the heat in his eyes.

"Well, I'm here now, so you can go." I tossed my purse onto the sofa and gestured toward the door.

"You're pissed." His bewilderment only served to make

me feel more foolish. I thought we had a connection, but maybe it was all in my head.

I blew out a deep breath and took a seat on the sofa. "I'm not pissed." A weird sense of exhaustion replaced all the anger I'd felt earlier. The thought of reliving the mental and emotional pain of another person leaving had stripped away all my energy and left nothing but numbness.

"Yeah, I'm pretty sure you're pissed. Is it because I haven't been around?" He glanced down at his feet and tugged his lower lip between his teeth, a gesture I found utterly sexy.

"Okay, yes, I was pissed at first, but I'm over it. You have a life to live out there." I waved a hand toward the picture window. "And my life is inside here with Hank."

"About that," he began, but I cut him off.

"Look, you don't get to just come in and out of our lives when you feel like it, without notice." The confession ignited my temper again, and all the pent-up frustration and hurt bubbled to the surface. I pointed a finger at him. "I don't want you here. Get out."

"Can we talk about this?"

I pushed at his chest with both hands, shoving him toward the door. "No. We can't talk about it."

He caught my hands by the wrist and held them down at my sides. My nipples tightened at his touch. I was angry with him, but apparently, my body hadn't gotten the message.

Abe arrived in time to stop me from shoving him again. "Hey, what's going on here?"

"I was just throwing Tucker out," I said, giving him my best glare. He released my hands but didn't back away.

Abe pursed his lips. I took his silence as mutiny, pivoted on my heel, and stormed upstairs to my bedroom. The door slammed behind me and rattled the pictures on the wall in the hallway. I hadn't done that since I was a teenager, and the act gave me little satisfaction five years later.

Thirty seconds passed before a tentative rap sounded at the door. I ignored it, choosing instead to flip through the pages of a technology magazine. I knew it was Tucker, and I had nothing to say to him. Instead, I buried my nose in an article, seeing nothing but red splotches.

"I hope you're decent, because I'm coming in."

I stared in disbelief as the door opened, and Tucker came into my private domain. No male, other than Hank and my father, had ever breached the threshold. I tossed a pillow at him. "Go away." He caught it deftly in one hand and tossed it back to me. "What is it with you?" I asked.

"I have a few things to say before I go, and you're going to listen."

"No." My lower lip began to quiver. Whatever he had to say, I wasn't interested in hearing it, because I knew he could change my mind with one touch, one word, one look from those soft hazel eyes. He was going to hurt me, and I had a feeling this time I wouldn't be able to recover. I held out a hand to ward him away. "I know where you were, what you did. I don't want any part of it."

"What are you talking about?" He frowned.

Tears blurred my eyes. How could I explain when I hardly understood myself? "You made me care about you, and then you go off and do something crazy like jump off a mountain. You could've been killed. I can't go through that again." The enormity of how close he'd come to dying broke down my last wall of defense. I buried my face in my hands. "I've already lost too much. So has Hank. We can't go through it again."

16

———

TUCKER

er anger hit me hard, like a percussion blast. The sight of tears spilling from her large, expressive eyes wrenched away the iron gate around my heart. "Hey, hey." I sat on the edge of the bed and put an arm around her shoulders. Each sob wracked her thin body. I pulled her head into my chest and stroked a hand through her hair. "I'm sorry. So sorry."

"I was crazy worried," she whispered, clinging to my shirt, fingers clenched in the cotton. "You might not care what happens to you, but other people do."

The ache filling my chest grew with every tear she shed. "Shhhh. It's okay. I'm right here. Nothing's going to happen to me."

My words acted like a catalyst, halting her sobs. She lifted her face. A tear clung to the point of her chin. "You don't know that."

"I do. It's perfectly safe. I've got over two hundred skydives under my belt. I'm trained." Even as I spouted excuses, doubt gnawed at my confidence. Caleb accused me of flirting with death, and maybe he was right.

"Accidents happen. I looked it up. Twenty-seven people died last year, and the numbers are climbing. Every time you jump, you take your life in your hands." The anguish in her eyes hurt more than her words. "My parents left the house on a Saturday evening, and they never came back. They were going two blocks down the street, to pick up a few things at the grocery. The guy who killed them only had two beers. He was on his way home from a family barbecue. Three people in the wrong place at the wrong time. It only takes a second for fate to intervene."

"I can't live my life in fear." Even though her story shook me to the core, I was too stubborn to listen, to hear the meaning behind her words. "Maybe you're happy living under a rock, but I'm not. There's a whole wide world out there for me to experience, and I'm going to grab it by the balls."

Crimson patches colored her cheeks. Fire sparked in her eyes. "Do you think I like being stuck in this house, day after day, year after year, knowing I have no future?" I reared back, shocked by the furious tremble of her voice. "Not everyone has the luxury of freedom. Some of us have people who rely on us, responsibilities." She waved her hands between us. "I do it because I love my brother, and I'd do anything to make him happy."

Shit. I dragged a hand over my face and drew in a deep breath. This conversation had taken an unpleasant turn. Uneasiness coursed through my veins. A fissure had opened between us. It split wider with each passing moment. I felt her slipping away from me. If I didn't do something quickly, we might never make our way back to each other.

"It doesn't have to be like that." I spoke slowly, choosing my words with care. "You shouldn't have to give up who you are to be with someone else." This conversation had nothing to do with Hank, and everything to do with Fallon and me.

"Life is precious, Tucker Spaulding, and you're squandering it. Don't you think Hank would give anything to be able to live a normal life? Just to walk out to the mailbox one more time? And here you are, able bodied with everything a man could ask for, and you're practically begging for fate to take it all away."

"It's what I do, Fallon. I take risks. I'm a gambler, an adrenalin junkie. I need the rush." I pushed a hand through my hair, shoving it out of my eyes, only to see her face pale with fear. "This is me."

"But it's not me." With both palms flat on my chest, she pushed away and shook her head. "Life is risky enough without taking chances. Hank needs to know you're going to be around tomorrow or the day after. He can't handle losing anyone else. You can risk your life if you want to, but I can't let you hurt Hank."

"I can't stop." No matter how hard I tried, I couldn't look at her, knowing my words caused her pain. "I'll never be the kind of man who works in an office wearing a suit and tie, who sits on the couch drinking beer after work every night. I live for the thrill." I stroked a fingertip over the velvety softness of her cheek. "I *need* the thrill."

Her voice softened so much I had to lean forward to hear what she said. "I hate the thrill."

"Then I guess we're at an impasse," I said. I stormed down the stairs, through the living room and onto the porch, letting the screen door slam shut behind me. I was too pissed, too broken to care about the buzzing of my phone inside my pocket. She wanted safety and complacence, two words absent from my vocabulary. Although I wanted to make her happy, I couldn't give her what I didn't possess.

Maybe it was best to go our separate ways now, like she suggested, before anyone got hurt. I already ached inside at the thought of never seeing her again.

My phone continued to buzz. Once I pulled into the driveway of my house, I scrolled through the list of texts and voice mails. Beckett left his sunglasses in my office. Sam needed the phone number of my chiropractor. Venetia wanted my approval on some changes to the design of my office. My grandma. Caleb. Roni. The last name on the list nearly stopped my heart. *Sydney*.

17

———

FALLON

On Monday morning, I went to work with a heavy heart and red, swollen eyes. As usual, I arrived an hour before everyone else. When eight o'clock rolled around, Andrew still hadn't shown up. I ran through my morning reports with one eye on the door and the other on his office. Something didn't feel right. At nine o'clock, security escorted Andrew to his office and watched while he packed his personal items into a brown cardboard box. Twenty minutes later, they walked him to the elevator.

My stomach turned over as the head of Human Resources and the Vice President of Accounting headed in my direction. I smoothed my skirt over my legs with shaking hands and tried to breathe. *Not now. Not today.* I couldn't handle another disappointment. I was already broken over Tucker.

"Can you come with us, please?" the VP asked.

I rose and followed them into Andrew's office. The VP shut the door behind us and nodded to a chair across from the desk. This was it. I was getting the axe. My thoughts raced as I tried to think how I might cover the bills until I could find another job. I'd have to let Abe go and maybe Hillary, too.

"Ms. Youngblood?"

"Yes?" My voice quavered. I lifted my chin, determined to handle the situation with dignity.

"We wanted to inform you that Andrew has been let go." Ms. Vincente, the Human Resources director, spoke in even, clipped tones.

My heart began a frantic pace and my mouth went dry. I stared at my toes and tried to concentrate on breathing. *It'll be okay. I'm strong. I can deal with this.*

"We've brought you in here because we'd like to offer you a temporary job as his replacement," the VP said.

My head snapped up. Was this for real? "Me?" I asked in a high, thin voice.

"Yes. Your dedication hasn't gone unnoticed. We're all very pleased with your work." Ms. Vincente smiled, and a little of my anxiety fell away.

"The job is yours, along with a ten percent salary increase. And we'd like to help you finish your degree through our tuition reimbursement program," the VP added. "Once you've graduated, you'll get another ten percent raise. And of course, you'll be eligible for yearly and quarterly bonuses, depending upon the performance of your department."

"Oh." I placed a hand on my chest to control my racing heart. After a short discussion, I signed the job offer and began moving my things into my new office. Once I was alone, I sat in the big chair behind my desk and wished I had someone to share the news with. And that someone was Tucker.

18

TUCKER

After the fight with Fallon, I threw myself into work with a passion for the next two weeks. I decided to research video game controls designed for quadriplegics, something that might benefit others like Hank. The work kept me busy during the days, but at night, my thoughts returned to Fallon. I missed her, and I missed Hank. Sometimes, I found myself driving by their house just to reassure myself it was still there, that they were okay.

Needing to dull some of the ache from Fallon's anger, I scheduled a jump. This one would be from a bridge spanning the Laurel River. Caleb had agreed to go along, probably because I'd shamed him into it, or to make sure I didn't do anything stupid.

As I climbed over the railing of the bridge and stood there, I waited for the heady flood of adrenalin, the crazy wild feeling of hovering between life and death. A light breeze ruffled my hair. At my feet, the river tumbled over boulders and fallen logs, churning and swirling. I fixated on the murky depths, anticipating the euphoria. I waited and waited, but it never came.

"You okay?" Caleb touched my arm, a frown on his face.

"I'm fine." I gripped the railing, staring down into the precipice and the flowing water far beneath us.

"Wind's good. Timing's perfect," Caleb said, interrupting my thoughts. "If you're going to go, do it now."

The cold steel of the bridge chilled my fingers. I closed my eyes and drew in a deep breath. The wind brushed my cheeks, soft like Fallon's caress. I thought about Fallon's smiles, her kiss, and her quiet strength. The water taunted me but held no answers.

I threw my legs over the railing and climbed back onto the road. My fingers fumbled over the straps of my gear. "I'm out of here, man," I told Caleb.

"What's up?" Caleb frowned at me.

"Never been better." I clapped him on the back. All this time, I'd been jumping to feel alive, to forget the past, but I had a future, and I didn't want to lose it over something as trivial as a jump. I'd never lose my love of extreme sports, but there were hundreds of other options in the world besides BASE jumping. I quickened my pace, leaving Caleb behind, scratching his head. I had a life to live. I still intended to live it to the fullest but with Fallon, if she'd have me. I didn't know where we were headed, or if we'd last, but I had to find out.

19

———

FALLON

Because I was now the manager of my department at Reyes Media, I had a little more flexibility in my hours. When the weekend came, a lawn service arrived to mow the yard, and my heart sank. I missed Tucker, but I wasn't sure I could deal with his love for doing wild and crazy things. It just wasn't me. I needed safe and reliable. Our separation was for the best. Neither Hank nor I needed the anguish. Even though my head agreed, my heart rebelled against the notion.

Another week passed. On the next Saturday, the weather languished, hot and miserably humid. Abe and Hank watched the latest baseball game, while I folded laundry on the kitchen table. Every time I thought about Tucker, anguish stabbed my heart. What was he doing? Did he miss me? I tried to rationalize a reason to talk to him but came up with nothing. I sighed and placed the folded bath towels into a basket for the upstairs bathroom. Maybe I'd been too hard on him. Then I shook my head. I kept going around in circles. One minute, I wanted to beg his forgiveness, and the next I knew we were through.

My phone vibrated on the coffee table with an incoming text. Abe rose from the couch and brought it into the kitchen. I stared at the caller ID.

Tucker: I miss you.

I stared at the phone, disbelieving. I read the text again, pressing my lips together, trying to decipher the hidden meaning. Did he miss me like a friend, or did he really miss me? The next message arrived on the heels of the first.

Tucker: I'm a douche.

I bit my lower lip to hold back a smile.

Tucker: Let me make it up to you. Give me a second chance.

With a thumb, I caressed the screen and his words. He missed me. My head told me to walk away before I got hurt. We had major issues to overcome. I couldn't just dismiss our differences. My heart, on the other hand, didn't care about any of those trivial things.

Me: What about our disagreement?

A full minute passed then two. I waited, breathlessly, scared to hope. Maybe he had changed his mind.

Tucker: I'm willing to compromise if you are.

Compromise? The word held new meaning. I didn't take risks, but this was a different situation. The idea of going another two weeks without him seemed impossible, let alone another day. If I didn't take a leap into the unknown, I'd be stuck in this house alone, forever. Is that what I wanted? To be alone with my mute brother for eternity? *No. No, no, no, no, no.* Before I could talk myself out of it, I punched in Tucker's number.

"Hey." His surprised voice answered on the first ring. The sound of the smooth tenor quieted my misgivings and unleashed a flood of adrenalin through my veins. I sat down on the nearest chair, unable to trust the integrity of my knees.

"Okay. I'm willing to talk about it." I covered my eyes with a hand. What was I doing? This could either be a huge mistake or an enormous blessing. Either way, I wasn't quite prepared for the consequences.

"I'm coming over. Don't go anywhere. I'll be there in an hour." He hung up before I could gather my courage to speak again.

An hour? I ran upstairs and began a rapid rescue mission for my appearance. By the time I'd pulled together an outfit and fixed my hair, the doorbell was ringing. Heat rocketed through my body. I opened the door to find Tucker standing on the doorstep with his hands shoved into the pockets of his over-washed jeans. His soft eyes smiled down at me, filled with uncertainty. I smiled back at him.

"Hi," I said, my voice breathy.

"Hey." He jerked his chin. His gaze roamed over me, like he hadn't seen me in months instead of weeks. My cheeks warmed under his appraisal. Something was different about his stance. He seemed taller, more confident. The mischievous twist of his lips sent my heart into an erratic, gleeful rhythm. "I've got a surprise for you and Hank," he said.

"Oh, really?" I asked. The playful tone of his voice sang in my ears and curled my toes inside my sandals. I'd missed him so much more than I cared to admit.

"Come and look." He took my hand and tugged me onto the porch. A crew of people stood around a brand-new, state-of-the-art wheelchair. Hillary and Les were there, too. I looked from Tucker to Hillary then back again, uncertain what to make of this revelation.

"We wanted to surprise you," Hillary said, her eyes brimming with tears. "Tucker set this up weeks ago."

"I don't know what to say." My own eyes threatened to spill tears as well. This one gift would open a world of opportunities for Hank and do wonders for his morale. No one had ever done anything so kind for us, and the gesture broke down my protective walls. I covered my face with my hands to hide the wealth of emotions I couldn't control.

"You don't have to say anything. We're happy to help." Venetia stepped forward from behind the crew and wrapped an arm around my shoulders. Hillary patted my back. I lowered my hands and noticed Sam and Beckett at the side. "The van is yours to keep, as well. It's fully equipped with a lift and completely handicap accessible."

"How is this possible? We can't take it. It's too much." Gratitude rushed through me like a warm tide, filling the cracks of my wounded heart. "I'll never be able to afford this." I looked to Tucker for answers and was surprised to see his expression soft and tender. Those beautiful lips curved into a smile.

"Venetia contacted a few local charities on your behalf," he said. "I told her you wouldn't mind." He reached out and swiped a tear from my cheek with the pad of his thumb.

"Beckett and Sam helped, too." Venetia touched my arm, her features lighting as she spoke on a topic she obviously loved. "And we'd like to talk with you about starting a charity in Hank's name to help others like him. We could really use your input."

"I think it's a lovely idea," I managed to say through the lump in my throat. I couldn't remember the last time anyone had done anything so thoughtful or so selfless for my brother. Tucker had been an instrumental part in this godsend. It made me love him all the more. How could I help it when he did things like this? I couldn't risk my heart over someone so reckless, so wild. Deep down, I knew it was too late. I'd fallen hard for him. Would I ever get over him if he didn't love me back?

"I'm going to hold you to your word," Venetia said. "There's a charity auction and dinner next weekend, and I'd love for you to come. Benefactors love to put a face to the name. It would mean a lot. I can introduce you to some of the people who want to help."

"Okay." The idea of rubbing shoulders with the city's most prominent citizens scrambled my insides, but it was the least I could do. "If you think it's important, I'll go."

"Let's get this inside so Hank can see it." Tucker jerked his chin toward the front door. I pushed my overwhelming emotions aside to give Hank the spotlight.

With Abe's help, Hank sat in his new wheelchair for the first time. Complicated technology allowed him to control the chair using a mouthpiece. I reveled in Hank's joy. As he wheeled around the living room, he bumped into the furniture, knocked over the lamp, and scuffed the wall, but it didn't matter. We cheered and laughed at each exciting new turn. Hank's eyes brightened, and his smile lit up my day.

"It'll take some getting used to," the wheelchair rep said to Hank before he left. "But you'll be moving around like a pro in no time." He handed his card to me. "If you have any questions, or need anything at all, please call my cell."

Hank nodded. His glowing smile said more than words. These wonderful people had given him a precious gift. Their generosity would allow him freedom, something he hadn't experienced since the accident, and a reason to go on. Hank wasn't the only one to receive a present; they'd restored my faith in goodness.

20

FALLON

Once everyone else had gone, I walked Tucker to his truck, teeming with endorphins. After the gift he'd given Hank, I was willing to overlook his reckless tendencies. Shoot, I'd overlook just about anything.

"You crazy, wonderful man," I said. Unable to contain my joy any longer, I threw my arms around his neck and squeezed him with all my strength. He stiffened, shocked by my uncharacteristic enthusiasm, then wrapped his arms around my waist and held me tight. I'd been going for more of a grateful hug, but there was nothing platonic in the way his hands caressed my back. The force of his embrace flattened my breasts against his chest and started a riot of butterflies in my stomach.

"It was nothing. V did all the work," he said, his voice reverberating in my ear. A blush heightened the sunburn across his cheeks.

"It's not nothing, Tucker. It's everything. You've given Hank a reason to wake up in the morning, and that alone is priceless. I'll never be able to repay you." My voice broke on the last word.

"Seeing Hank smile was payment enough," he said and let his hands slide down over the curve of my hips.

The stubble of his cheek scratched my lips. I felt the rise and fall of his ribs with each breath, the pounding of his heart against my breasts. His nose grazed my hair as he took a deep breath, scenting me. The primal maleness of this act sent a bolt of wetness straight into my panties.

"God, I missed you." He tightened his hold. "Does this mean you're not mad at me anymore?"

I snuggled into the curve of his neck, hoping he wouldn't let go. "I'm not mad."

"We need to talk." He lifted a hand to toy with the ends of my hair while the other continued to splay over my back. "There's something I've got to tell you."

"I don't like the sound of that." I leaned away to get a better look at his face. His eyes searched mine, their hazel color bordering on brown.

"After we argued, I went to make another jump," he said. The contents of my lunch churned in my gut at the thought of the enormous bridge and the long drop to the river below. I looked down, but he cupped my chin and lifted my face. "I had every intention of throwing myself off the bridge, but all I could think of was you."

"Me?" The moisture left my mouth as his eyes dipped to my lips. "Why?"

"I realized my reasons for jumping had changed. It wasn't worth the risk." His thumb swept over my lower lip. "It wasn't worth losing you."

21

TUCKER

Twilight beckoned on the horizon of Fallon's neighborhood. We stood at the street next to my truck, her arms around my neck, my hands gripping her waist. No matter how hard I tried, I couldn't let her go.

The heat of her body pressed to mine, the sweet puff of her breath against my neck, and the scent of her hair tightened all the muscles in my groin. Sweet Jesus, she smelled good, like honey and fresh air and soap. I couldn't stop smelling her hair, to the point it kind of scared me. She probably thought I was some kind of weirdo.

Sydney became more of a faded photograph instead of the crystal-clear snapshot she'd once been. A memory was hard pressed to compete with the feel of a living, flesh-and-blood girl like Fallon. She was soft and warm and filled the lonely, aching void left by Sydney. The way Fallon's eyes lit up when she saw me, her rare but infectious laughter, and the haunting beauty of her face tugged at my heartstrings. And when she smiled? God, it was like watching a rainbow after a thunderstorm, the rush comparable to the highest BASE jump.

"You like to do wild things. I don't want to change who you are," she said.

"I'll still do wild things." I smiled down at her. She was selfless, always putting someone else's happiness in front of her own. "I just won't be so reckless."

"Maybe you can teach me to be a little bit wild, too." She bit into the fullness of her bottom lip. The gesture caused a yearning low in the pit of my belly.

"Deal."

Her fingers tangled in my hair. When I looked down into her amazing gold eyes, all I could think about was how she might taste, and how badly I wanted to pull her full lower lip between my teeth. Her gaze went to my lips then rebounded back up to my eyes. I traced the dimple on her cheek with my thumb. The rapid tattoo of her heart against my sternum reminded me how much I'd missed being close to a girl, how lonely I'd been. Our mouths inched closer until her lips melted against mine.

The wet heat of her tongue slid over mine and released a desire I hadn't experienced before. I backed her against the truck, trapping her hips between the fender and my pelvis, and pushed into her. She lifted one of her legs and wrapped it around my thigh.

The kiss went from tentative to demanding in the space of a breath. We were a cluster of desperate lips and clutching fingers. I wanted to lay her back, spread her long legs, and see if I could make her cry out my name. One of my hands slid down her hip, grabbed a handful of her bottom, and claimed her as mine.

"Tucker." I heard my name from far away. My mouth

sucked at the sweet flesh beneath her ear. Her hand cupped my jaw. "Tucker. Please."

"What?" My voice came out hoarse and guttural. I drew in a deep breath and tried to center my thoughts.

"Tucker, we're in public. On the street. People can see us." She laughed a little and shuddered when I nipped at her earlobe.

"Right." The throbbing in my cock made it difficult to think. I released her bottom and put enough space between us to see her kiss-swollen lips.

"We could go back inside," she said hopefully. "Hank's asleep, and Hillary goes to bed early."

I yearned for the feel of heated flesh on flesh, the soothing touch of a woman who cared for me and whom I was beginning to care for in return. I pushed aside the uncertainty, took Fallon's hand, and gave her a smile. There was nowhere I'd rather be than with her.

22

———

FALLON

Tucker's mouth sucked on the curve of my neck where my shoulder and collarbone met. We were in the basement. I came down here now and then when I needed to get away but couldn't leave the house. It reminded me of Dad, the warm wood paneling, the over-stuffed sofa, and a few of his things still strewn about. I hadn't been able to part with his pipe or the pair of reading glasses resting next to an open book on the coffee table.

I stroked a hand down Tucker's flat stomach to grip the growing bulge behind the fly of his jeans. He groaned and pressed into my palm. "Shhhh. You'll wake up the house," I warned, biting back a smile.

"I feel like a teenager on prom night," he whispered into my ear. One of his hands teased the strip of bare skin between my tank top and shorts. "I haven't had to sneak around in a very long time."

"We're not sneaking." I gave him a playful shove.

He caught my hand and returned it to his crotch. "Sure feels like it to me." His other hand slipped beneath my shirt to cup my breast. "But I like it. It makes me feel dirty."

"I like it, too." I leaned back against the couch to give him better access. He lifted my shirt and tugged my bra cup down to take my nipple in his mouth. The sharp sting of his teeth sent a bolt of white-hot lust straight between my thighs.

"It's been a long time for me," he said. The raw emotion in his voice suggested how difficult it was for him to make the confession. "A very long time since I wanted to be with someone."

"Me, too." Hearing the vulnerability of his words eased some of my insecurities. I squirmed against his hot breath and the suction of his lips. Delicious spikes of pleasure vibrated down my legs.

"Did you love him?" The feel of his fingers slipping into my panties shot my concentration to hell.

"I thought so, but he didn't love me back." It was the first time I'd said the words aloud to anyone but myself, and it didn't hurt nearly as much as I thought it would. Time had provided clarity, and I could see now that Cody had never been as invested in our relationship as I'd been. The burden of Hank's accident would test the strongest of couples. "I think the whole deal with Hank was too much for him. Then he just quit coming around. I can't say that I blame him."

Tucker pushed back enough to look at me. "It's his loss. Don't ever doubt that."

His index finger circled my clit, slipping easily through the slick flesh. I hissed in pleasure and lifted my hips, needing more. In the moonlight streaming through the basement windows, the lines of his profile stood out in stark relief, sharp and clean. I tangled my fingers in the thickness of his hair and tugged. He growled.

"You're playing with fire. Do that again, and I'll have to

fuck you here, like this," he warned, his voice dangerously deep and low. "With your panties around your ankles and your legs on my shoulders."

"I like fire." I pulled his hair again, harder this time. Something about him made me feel wild, reckless, wanton. I angled his head and sucked hard on his neck.

With a sweeping motion, he yanked my shorts and panties to mid-thigh, baring me to him. He grazed his fingers through the short pubic curls between my thighs. "This is nice." He tugged on the hair, sending jolts of desire into places previously forgotten.

"Oh." The heat of embarrassment climbed into my cheeks. I hadn't bothered with trimming the hedges in a long time. What was the point when I had no intentions of having sex? I tried to cover myself with my hands, but he captured them by the wrists and pulled them away.

"No, no. No, you don't. I like a full bush." Two dimples popped in each cheek and his eyes sparkled with humor. "Wild thing."

"Don't tease me." I already felt inadequate next to his sexy hotness, knowing his former girlfriend was famous for her risqué Instagram photos.

"I'm not teasing. I like it." He released my hands and stroked between my legs again. I moaned as need tightened in the pit of my belly. "And I like the little noises you make."

We kissed until my lips ached, and my pussy throbbed. Every time I tried to unzip his fly, he blocked my fingers. At the same time, he continued to tease and taunt the swollen flesh between my legs. He flicked my clit, and a wave of unexpected pleasure rolled through my limbs. I squirmed, trying to get away and get closer at the same time. Too many strong sensations sent my mind spinning.

"Will you come for me?" The tip of his tongue skated over my earlobe. His breath scorched my ear.

"Ah, yes." I nuzzled my nose against his neck. "I'm close."

"I want to hear you moan. You're so wet, Fallon." His middle finger pushed inside me. Combined with the pressure of his thumb, those two fingers drove me to the edge and held me there. My legs tightened and trembled. The heat and quake of an orgasm began to ball up in my core. I drew in a shuddering breath and clutched his back, raking him with my nails in a desperate attempt to keep my precious control, to stay quiet. He slipped a second finger inside me, curled it upward, and hit the sweet spot. I bit my lip, stifling a cry, my orgasm rippling over his hand.

"I want you," I said, louder than I should have, heedless of the sleeping people upstairs. I wriggled against him, desperate to have him inside me, crazed by the lingering effects of my climax. "Inside me. Oh, God. Inside me. Right now. Do you have a condom?"

"Yes. I think so. Hang on." He sat up to dig through his wallet. After an eternal minute, he held up a foil packet between index and middle fingers. I breathed a sigh of relief. I hadn't owned a condom for years, and I wasn't on the pill. After Cody had left, there hadn't been any need for it. He pushed the packet into my hand. "Put it on me."

I stared at the packet, my hands trembling, while he tugged my clothing down my legs. This wasn't like me. I didn't do things like this, but it seemed so right, so dangerous, so naughty. I straddled his thighs and paused long enough to glance up at his face. His eyes were dark, shadowed by long lashes, heavy-lidded. After a deep inhale, I ripped the packet open with my teeth.

Tucker eased the zipper of his fly over the huge bulge beneath. He lifted up from the couch to pull the faded denim jeans down to his knees. Coarse hair dusted thighs thick with muscle. Long fingers gripped the base of his cock, holding it upright. The flesh below his belly button was pale and smooth, the skin above tanned to a golden brown. Excitement buzzed from the top of my head through my body and into my toes.

"I'm not very good at this," I said in a whispery voice. I placed the condom over the head of his cock and smoothed it over the tip, using both hands to pull it down the length of his shaft. He groaned and pushed upward into my hand. His eyes closed and his head tipped back. The Adam's apple in his throat bobbed. When he opened his eyes, they were filled with piercing heat.

"You did fine. Now come here." With a hand on each of my hips, he pulled me forward. "Guide me in."

Without breaking eye contact, I raised on my knees, enough to allow him access. His fingers curled into the flesh of my bottom and pushed me down onto him. He sank inside me with a prolonged moan. His cock was thick and hard and consumed me. Neither of us moved. Neither of us blinked. A kaleidoscope of colors flecked his hazel eyes; green, gold, brown, blue. They held absolute power over me. I saw a history of pain inside them, a man with a sensitive soul, and a generous heart. Could he see inside me, the secrets and pain I kept locked away?

He shifted and drove deeper. I winced as he nudged my womb.

"You okay?" he asked, his voice textured. I nodded. "It's good, isn't it?"

"Yes." It was better than good; it was amazing, spectacular, mind-blowing. I lifted up, hissing at the friction between us, before sliding down the length of his cock. "Do you like it?"

"Baby," was all he said. He leaned forward to take my mouth, caressing his hands up and down my back. Our tongues tangled, while our hips jerked and rocked. It was slow and intense, easy but strange, wild and carnal.

Tucker countered each of my movements with one of his own. I lost control of my motions and rode him with ferocious abandon. I no longer cared how I looked or if I was doing it right, consumed with the need to climax. Our flesh slapped together. I gripped his shoulders for balance and increased the pace until the sofa rocked on its legs.

There was a certain amount of power in riding him. From my seat on top, I controlled the speed and depth of his thrusts, the angle of his entry, and the timing of our orgasms. Cody had always been on top and negligent of my pleasure. Tucker swept my shirt over my head and tossed it aside. His palms squeezed my breasts. He bent forward to take one nipple between his teeth. The sharp sting of pleasure-pain rippled all the way to my toes.

"Fallon, what are you doing to me?" He took my jaw in his hand and angled my face to his. The raw emotion in his voice brought a prickle of tears to my eyes. "You feel so good, so right."

The final barrier around my heart disintegrated into a thousand pieces. I loved this man with all my being. The words hovered on the tip of my tongue. I bit them back. What if he didn't love me back? Was it too soon? I didn't want to ruin the moment by rushing him.

His arms wrapped around my waist, and he flipped us onto the floor. I rested on my back, the wool rug prickly against my bare skin. Tucker raised my knee to his waist with one hand while balancing on the opposite elbow. He began to drive into me over and over and over. The force of his penetration caused the walls of my pussy to contract around him.

When I cried out, he slowed the pace, moving with deliberation, wringing out the length of my orgasm, prolonging the pleasure until my body went limp. Then he came inside me. I knew by his staccato grunts, the way his fingers dug into my breast, the ragged edge of his breathing, and the jerk of his body between my legs. The overwhelming intimacy took me by surprise. He was inside me, deep and steady. Our heartbeats mingled until I couldn't tell where my pulse ended and his began.

We lay still in the quiet for a long time afterward, his body on top of me, our legs tangled, chests heaving. His fingers soothed up and down my ribs. I remained still, unwilling to break the magic of the moment, afraid it was all a dream. Good things didn't happen to me, and when they did, fate always stepped in to ruin it.

"I'm not sure how we do this," he whispered into my ear. "What I feel for you, it scares the living shit out of me. I just need to go slow, okay?"

I nodded.

"Sydney—she fucked me up." He brushed the hair from my face and pressed a kiss into the hollow of my throat. "I'm not sure if I'll ever be the same."

I swallowed down the taste of jealousy, dry as sawdust. "You still love her?" The words made my throat ache.

"No." He shifted to look into my eyes. "I'm not sure it was ever love. I mean, how can love be so ugly?" The anguish in his voice struck a chord within me. I knew how it felt to lose someone you loved, to cling desperately to the frayed remnants of their memories, and the confusion of their betrayal.

"Shhhh. Tucker, it's okay." I forgot about my humiliation in the face of his pain. "Come here."

He'd done so much for me, for Hank. The least I could do was give back a little of the kindness he'd shown us. I cupped his face in my hands and forced him to look at me. The anguish in his long-lashed eyes split my heart in two. He wrapped his arms around my waist. I pulled him into me, cuddling his face into my neck, and soothed a hand down the grooves of his back.

"You can talk to me about her, if you want," I offered. Although I was jealous of this girl, someone I'd never have the chance to meet, I wanted to help him. The fewer secrets between us, the stronger our relationship.

"Things—they were complicated," he said after a pause so long, I thought he might have fallen asleep. "She was always focused on her career. We had to sneak around to avoid the tabloids. I never got to go anywhere in public with her." The remorse was palpable in his voice. "And she never really broke up with me. I saw her wedding on the TV."

"That's inexcusable," I said, my anger growing at the idea of a woman toying with him, taking his generous heart for granted. "You didn't deserve that."

"Maybe not. But I was an idiot for thinking we had something serious." His lips brushed over my jaw. "You don't have a fiancé hiding in the closet, do you?"

"No." We both laughed. The weight of his head on my breast felt good, like it belonged there. I toyed with the hair at the nape of his neck.

"Do you ever think about your parents?" he asked.

"All the time. Not as much as I used to, but sometimes, in the early morning, when I'm half asleep, I hear my mom moving around in the kitchen, my dad's voice as he reads something in the paper to her." Remembering brought an ache to my chest. I cleared my throat, wanting to share their memories, willing to endure the pain if it helped him share his own. "They were good people. My mom was really sweet and funny. She used to make us pancakes shaped like hearts." His lips pressed a kiss against my breast. "And my dad liked to chase us around the house, making us squeal. We were happy." For the first time since their deaths, I felt the joy of their lives instead of the pain that came after. As I stroked a hand through Tucker's hair, I realized my parent's memories could bring me happiness as well as pain; the choice was up to me.

23

———

TUCKER

The sound of a dog barking woke me from the best sleep I'd had in a year. Something heavy crushed my chest. I opened my eyes to find Fallon draped over my torso, her arms wrapped around my middle, and her head pillowed in the crook of my neck. My back ached from the lumpy sofa, but I hesitated to move. It felt too good lying there with her, the cool morning breeze wafting through the open basement window.

When I tried to move, she stirred and stretched, lazy and languid like a cat. Her eyes fluttered open, and she smiled up at me. My pulse skipped a beat. I smiled back at her and brushed a stray lock of hair from her forehead. Her eyes glowed in the morning light. My hand went to the back of her neck and cupped her nape.

"Good morning," she said, her voice thick with sleep.

"Morning." Unable to resist her kiss-swollen lips, I pulled her mouth to mine. My head spun with the taste of her sweetness. We pulled apart, and I reached to adjust myself, my cock jumping to full alert.

"What time is it?" She yawned and batted soft eyes at

me. Those gold irises turned me inside out. I felt raw and vulnerable. She got to me in a way no one else could or ever had, and it scared me.

"It's early." I ran a hand through my hair. "I've got to get out of here before Hillary or Hank wakes up." I shoved my feet into my shoes and shuffled toward the door then stopped. What the hell was I doing? This sweet, gorgeous girl wanted me, and by God, I wanted her, too. I turned to face her. "Do you like the water?"

She sat up and moistened her lips with her tongue before speaking. A puddle of sunshine illuminated the highlights in her hair. I'd never seen anyone so sexy, so vulnerable. The look of trust in her eyes slayed me. "I guess so," she said. "Why?"

A smile curved my mouth, the sensation foreign but welcome. "Well, it's supposed to be really nice today. I thought we might go out on my boat."

She studied me, lower lip drawn between her teeth, and tilted her head to one side. "You have a boat?"

"I do. A small one. And I'm thinking it would look a whole lot better with you on the deck." My head swam with possibilities for the day. Being with Fallon felt good—right. I wanted to take her someplace nice, show her a good time, make her smile some more. And then, later, I was going to take her back to my place and make love to her.

"Yeah. Sure." She smiled, and something caught in my chest. I rubbed my sternum to ease the tightness. Was that what I wanted? To make love to her? *No.* I scrubbed a hand over my face. *Yes.* I wanted to hear her scream with pleasure, feel her fingers rake down my back in ecstasy. Nothing seemed more important than making her happy, and I couldn't wait to get started. What we did last night was more than sex, it had meant something.

"I'll call you later, okay?" I dropped a kiss on her forehead.

She kneeled on the sofa in front of me and wrapped her arms around my neck. The dark circles of her nipples shone through the thin cotton of her T-shirt. "Okay, but you could stay for breakfast. Hank and Hillary won't mind."

The heat of her flesh warmed my palm as I swept a hand down her back to grab a handful of her bare bottom. I groaned. Sitting at the kitchen table with her sounded like a fucking dream come true. "I can't. I'm out of town next week. I haven't even packed yet."

"Fine." She sat back on her heels and smoothed her palms over my chest. I caught one of her hands in mine and pressed a kiss to her knuckles. "But don't take too long, okay?"

Her fingertips trailed through mine as I pulled away. I whistled a nameless tune on the way to my car. My feet floated above the ground. Dew drops sparkled on the green lawn, and sleepy quiet blanketed the neighborhood. Giddiness twisted my mouth into a goofy grin. I opened the door of the car and slid inside, enjoying the new car scent, the sunshine, and the promise of a beautiful day.

Before starting the car, I paused to scroll through a dozen missed calls and texts. The last name on the list caught my eye. Sydney. My guts knotted. I hovered a thumb over the message. I hadn't thought about her in days and didn't care to start now, when I'd just begun to put together the jagged shards of my heart. What did she want? In my opinion, we had nothing to say to each other. The bridge between us had been burned to cinders. I had deleted all her other messages, unread. Against my better judgment, I opened the text.

Sydney: I miss you. Call me.

Five little words carried the impact of a bulldozer. I tried to read the message hidden in the spaces between the words. My emotions swayed between curiosity and anger. Since our breakup, I'd been dying to know the reason for her defection. I'd dreamed of her calling to say she'd made a mistake, that it was some kind of misunderstanding, that she wanted me back. I stared at the phone then at Fallon's house. I could see her silhouette gliding past the curtains of her bedroom window as she got ready for the day. My legs and abs ached from fucking her, and I couldn't wait to do it again.

A neighbor cut in front of my car to check his mailbox. His Golden Retriever trailed on his heels. The open edges of his bathrobe flapped in the breeze to reveal print pajamas. He stopped to stare at me, eyes narrowed. I lifted a hand to wave, and he waved back, his features relaxing into a friendly smile. Sydney would never live in a neighborhood like this, but I would. Fallon would. I wanted that—a normal life, kids—with a woman who loved me.

24

FALLON

Tucker dropped anchor in a secluded cove of Laurel Lake. Tall trees bordered the shore, their heavy limbs dipping to the water, obscuring the cliffs from sight. A hot summer breeze rippled across the lake. Light waves lapped at the hull of the boat. I stretched out on a chaise and resisted the urge to pinch myself. If you'd told me two months ago that I'd be on the lake with Tucker Spaulding, I would have laughed in your face. Now, it seemed natural, right. I bit my lower lip to hold back a goofy grin.

So this is what it feels like to be happy. It had been so long, I'd forgotten.

Once the boat had been secured, he took the chair next to me and stretched his long legs in front of us. Behind my sunglasses, I admired the flex of his thighs, and the contrast of his tanned bare feet against the boat's blinding white deck. The muscles below my waist squeezed at the memory of his hard body on top of mine, the way he pounded into me. Every inch of my body ached from the unaccustomed workout. He glanced over at me and smiled. The space between my legs throbbed. I smiled back.

While I indulged in a new romance novel, he answered emails on his laptop. Comfortable silence filled the space between us. He pulled his shirt over his head and tossed it onto a nearby chair. My eyes drifted over his chest. He had just enough hair there, enough to curl my fingers in. Unlike me, he was bronzed all over, skin smooth and glowing. A pink hue already threatened my milky white skin. Dozens of freckles promised to follow. I drew a bottle of maximum sunblock from my tote bag.

"Need some help with that?" He nodded toward the bottle.

"Yes. Do you mind? I'll fry." The reflection of the scorching sun on the water promised a world of pain tomorrow if I didn't take proper precautions.

"Scooch up." He took the bottle and straddled the chaise behind me. "Take this off." His fingers tugged at the string tie at my nape, the one holding up the top of my romper suit. When I hesitated, he leaned forward, lips brushing my ear, sending shivers up my neck. "It's okay to show me your bikini. I was inside you last night."

A jumble of anxiety sucked the moisture from my mouth. I stood and untied the knot. While he watched, I let the halter top fall then pushed the shorts down over my hips to reveal my blue bikini. His gaze roamed over my bare skin, slid down my torso and lingered on the length of my legs. I shifted nervously. I hadn't worn a bathing suit in a long time, not since Hank's accident. The blatant appreciation in his eyes renewed my confidence.

He patted the seat in front of him, and I resumed my place between his legs. I flinched when his fingers glided over my neck. I still hadn't grown accustomed to the touch of another person. "Relax," he murmured in my ear.

With a steady hand, he slathered the cool lotion over my shoulders and back. He smoothed his palms over my tummy then along the length of my thighs. I sighed in pleasure. The gentle rocking of the boat combined with the touch of his hands made my eyelids heavy. My thoughts drifted, and my mind eased into a dreamlike state. It was perfect, too idyllic to be true.

"This is nice," I said. He leaned back and drew me with him. I rested my hands on top of his legs. His bare chest felt solid beneath me. Perspiration sprang up between us, but I didn't want to move. "Thanks for inviting me today. When you said you had a boat, I thought you meant a little boat. This is more like a yacht."

His chuckle reverberated against my back. "It's not a yacht. It's a motorboat. I do have a sailboat, though. At the marina in Key West. You should go there with me sometime." As he spoke, his lips brushed my hair. "You'd love it. I can teach you to ski."

"Maybe." My eyelids drifted shut. I focused on the rise and fall of his ribs and the beat of his heart. With his strong arms wrapped around my waist, it was easy to forget the weight of my responsibilities at home, about Hank and work.

"I really like you, Fallon." His confession caught me off guard. My pulse leaped.

"Oh?" The word stuck in my throat. I swallowed against the lump.

"Really, *really* like you." The softness of his lips nibbled my ear. I tilted my head to give him better access.

"I like you, too." I tried to breathe through the panic. I never considered that he might like me back. Not really.

Only in my dreams. Hearing him say the words aloud made the possibility real.

"I want you to be my girlfriend." He placed a fingertip beneath my chin and angled my face up to his. I couldn't see his eyes behind his sunglasses, but his lips curved in a smile.

"Okay." My breathing sounded harsh, like I'd been running up hill. "Sounds good to me," I replied and skated a palm along the outside of his leg. We shifted and touched lips. A tremor of excitement shook my body. In the space of a weekend, my life had taken on new shape, bursting with possibilities.

"Good." He slid his nose alongside mine and nuzzled the tip. Our lips met. His tongue, tasting of peppermint, dipped into my mouth, tentative and sweet.

"Mmmm." I hummed in approval. A bubble threatened to burst inside my chest. Life kept getting better with every passing second.

"I'm going to make love to you so hard," he whispered. Our fingers tangled together. "You need to get with your doctor for birth control, so I can fuck you bare. Not tonight. I'm heading to L.A. for the week, but I'll be back for the charity event on Saturday. You can be my date." He touched the tip of my nose with his. "And when it's over, I'm going to kiss all of your pink parts."

"Tucker Spaulding, you surprise me." The intimate tone of his voice caused moisture to pool between my legs.

"Why? Because I'm not afraid to tell you what I want from you?" One of his hands drifted over my breast and squeezed. "I've never had sex without a condom. I want you to be the first. I want to feel you from the inside, know your body, every inch of it." His hand skimmed down my tummy to press between my legs. "I want this to be mine."

I wasn't used to discussing the details of sex with a guy. Cody had always left the issue of protection to me, and there hadn't been anyone after him. I twitched my thighs together and shifted toward Tucker. Wanton need unfurled deep in my belly. He pushed his sunglasses onto his head. The bright sunlight transformed his hazel irises into pools of mossy green.

"I'll make an appointment on Monday," I said. The idea of visiting the gynecologist had never been more appealing.

We smiled at each other. He moved back to his chair but kept the fingers of his left hand entwined with my right. Our clasped hands formed a bridge across the space between us.

"You need to tell me what you want, what you need from me." He leaned forward and gripped my chin in his free hand, locking my gaze to his. "Do you understand?" I couldn't speak so I nodded. "Because I'll give you anything within my power, anything you want. Let me take care of you, Fallon."

Blood thundered through my ears. His words intoxicated me. Someone wanted to take care of *me*. It had been so long since anyone had my back. I had no idea how crushing the burden had been until the weight of responsibility slipped from my shoulders. I nearly cried out from the relief.

"I don't need you to take care of me, Tucker." The offer was enough. Even though he'd met Hank and seen the amount of care he required, I could never hold someone to such a promise.

"Maybe not." A smirk tipped up the corners of his mouth. "But I'm going to do it anyway."

We fell silent for a time. Lazy clouds drifted through the pale blue sky. When the sun reached its highest point, the heat became unbearable. Tucker stood then pulled me to my feet. "Come on." With his fingers threaded through mine, he tugged me toward the edge of the boat.

"Wait. What are you doing?" I shrank back, uncertain.

"Going for a swim." He released my hand and in a graceful motion, dived into the water. After a few pulse pounding seconds, he surfaced a dozen yards away. He shook his head, flinging drops of water in every direction. "It's okay. The water's deep. I'll be right here. I've got you."

His words meant everything to me, and I had no doubt he spoke from the heart. I wasn't the kind of girl who did reckless things, but the playful light in his eyes made me forget who I had been. He splashed a hand across the water and grinned. I drew in a deep breath, tossed aside my reservations, and plunged over the side.

25

FALLON

Thirty minutes later, we dragged back into the boat, exhausted but laughing. Tucker rubbed the water from my hair with a fluffy towel. I liked the way he thought of me first, how he tried to anticipate my needs. It felt good to have someone else in charge, to not have to think every single minute. As he dried my arms, his eyes darkened. The towel dropped to the deck. My nipples protruded through the wet triangles of my top. He flicked his thumbs over them. I hissed at the pleasurable sting.

"I like this." He gave a gentle tug to the bow holding my biking together on my left hip. "But I think I'd like it better on the floor." His hand went to my right hip, and he twisted a finger in the string. Mischief lit his eyes.

"Tucker." I grabbed his hand. Heat rushed into my cheeks.

"Just so you know, if you're my girlfriend, we're going to fuck. A lot." He yanked the string, untying the bow. His hot gaze drifted down my body, and I felt it like a touch.

I held the pieces of the bikini bottom together and rolled my eyes. "Seriously! Someone might see us."

"Hmmm. True." His palms smoothed beneath the fabric of my bikini and grabbed a handful of each butt cheek. His tight grip caused my muscles to clench deep between my legs. "Let's go below."

Before I could agree, the roar of an approaching boat had us scrambling. Tucker wrapped a towel around his waist to hide his erection while I retied the string on my hip. The driver reversed the engine. As the vessel came closer, I flattened a hand over my eyes to check out our visitors. Sam sat behind the wheel of a giant boat. Venetia and Beckett stood on the upper deck, and two women I didn't know sat behind Sam. Tucker slipped an arm around my waist and pulled me into his side.

"What's up, man?" Tucker called out to his friends as the boat idled next to us.

Sam's boat was twice the size of Tucker's, with two decks and a cabin below. Reggae music poured from hidden speakers. Beckett and Sam looked tan and fit in board shorts, shirtless, their hair mussed from the wind. Venetia wore an immaculate white one-piece suit. It was hard to believe she'd had a baby three months ago. I tightened the towel around my waist to hide my plain bikini and my stick-straight figure.

"I knew we'd find you here." Sam smiled, his eyes hidden behind mirrored aviators.

"Permission to come aboard, sir?" Beckett opened a cooler at his feet and removed a beer. He tossed it through the air. Tucker caught it with one hand, his opposite arm still around my waist.

"I told you we shouldn't sneak up on them. Maybe they don't want company." Venetia frowned at Beckett. "Sorry, Fallon. Boys will be boys."

My gaze drifted to the woman at Sam's elbow. He tugged her onto his lap. "Fallon, this is my wife, Dakota."

"It's nice to meet you," she said. My eyes met hers, and I was struck by the profound sadness in their depths. She tucked a strand of wavy brown hair behind her ear and mustered a weak smile. "I've heard a lot about you. Good things."

"Hi." I lifted a hand to wave when the third woman stepped forward. Tucker tensed. The breath rushed out of my lungs, like I'd been punched in the gut.

"Hey, Tucker," she said, eyes glued to him. I knew who she was without an introduction. Her golden skin glowed in the sunlight. Complicated strings held together tiny triangles of fiery red fabric on a body toned to perfection.

"Hey," Tucker said. His hand fell from my waist.

Sexual chemistry pulsed between them. Tucker moved to stand next to the railing. He popped the top of his beer and took a long guzzle. Sydney watched him through heavy-lidded eyes. She was beautiful on television but even more flawless in person. Her blue-black hair swung over her shoulders when she moved, a picture of sensual grace. After a beat, her eyes fell on me.

"Aren't you going to introduce me to your friend?" she asked. Everyone else faded into the background, until there was only Tucker, Sydney, and me. I wanted to look away or put my hands over my ears to block out their conversation, but I couldn't.

"Syd, this is Fallon. Fallon, meet Syd." The tension in his voice inflamed my discomfort.

A sour taste lingered on my tongue, but I managed to speak. "Hello." I couldn't say it was nice to meet her because it wasn't. My knuckles ached as I gripped the edges of my towel together. This was the girl who'd broken his heart. He'd been inside her. He'd loved her. Maybe he still loved her. I couldn't blame him, if he did. They both exuded charismatic, vibrant energy. The mental image of them together—two wild and beautiful creatures—turned my stomach.

"Fallon, it's a pleasure." Her gaze flicked back to Tucker, a soft smile on her pouty lips. "You didn't mention you were seeing someone."

From her statement, they were talking to each other, a tidbit he'd failed to mention. The knowledge stabbed me in the heart. I tried to breathe through feelings of jealousy and betrayal. *Stay calm, Fallon. You don't know the whole story.*

"And you didn't mention you were going to marry someone else." He took another drink of his beer, eyes drilling into her. I analyzed his tone in desperation, looking for a clue as to his state of mind. The steel edge of his voice suggested anger. I tried to shore up my self-confidence. He'd asked me to be his girlfriend, but I sure couldn't tell from the distance he'd put between us.

"Well, I guess we're even then." One of her dimples deepened with her smile.

"Not by a long shot," Tucker replied. He dropped the empty beer can into the trash bin at his feet then put an arm around my waist and pulled me into his side. I tensed, but didn't move away. I didn't want Sydney to see how her presence had twisted my feelings.

Someone cleared his throat. My attention snapped back to the others. Beckett shifted from one foot to the other. Sam lifted his eyebrows. No one met my gaze.

Venetia scowled at Sydney. "Syd, you promised to be nice."

"I *am* being nice." She frowned at her friend. A pink flush crawled up her neck and into her cheeks. Her focus returned to me. "I'm sorry." Her mouth twisted, and she looked down at her feet. "Sorry." She was a good actress. Her charade might fool the others, but I didn't believe it for one minute.

Once the initial shock of Sydney's appearance had faded, my feelings shifted toward anger. I leaned away from Tucker. His grip tightened around my waist. I resisted the urge to shove him and demand answers. They were talking to each other. Wasn't that something a girlfriend should know?

"Okay, well, I'm thinking we should be on our way." Dakota spoke for the first time since our introduction. I gave her a grateful glance. She nodded in reply.

"Great idea." Sam started the engine. "Tuck, we'll catch you later." The others waved goodbye. Sydney continued to stare at Tucker. The line of his jaw squared. I'd never seen him look so hard, so remote.

As soon as their boat circled around toward the mouth of the cove, I pushed Tucker aside. Unable to contain my irritation, I asked, "Are you using me to get back at her?" Tucker said nothing. The muscles in his throat worked as he swallowed. I took his silence to mean guilt. Tears pricked my eyes. I blinked them back and lifted my chin. After a painful pause, he blew out a heavy sigh and sank into one of the deck chairs. I dropped my towel and began shoving my feet into the romper suit. "I'd like to go home now, please."

"I'm not like that, Fallon, and if you think I am, you don't know me at all." Weariness increased his southern drawl. He blinked up at me. My heart squeezed at the depths of lingering hurt and shock in his eyes.

"Did you see her this morning?" In spite of my sympathy, he wasn't getting off without an explanation.

"No." He reached for my hand, but I snatched it back. His shoulders dropped, and he slumped deeper into the chair. An angry furrow darkened his brow. "She called me."

"After you fucked me? You talked to her?" Red orbs of jealousy floated in my vision. I yanked the romper top over my breasts and tied the string behind my neck. "Is *she* what you have to do this evening?"

"It's not like that." He jumped to his feet and grabbed my arm. I glared at him. His fingers tightened on my bicep. "She's been texting me, leaving voice mails. I texted her back this morning to say I was busy, but I haven't talked to her."

A little of the steam dissipated from my fury. I wanted to believe him with all my heart, but I'd been burned before. "You should have told me."

"I was going to tell you. Jesus." He released my arm and scrubbed both hands through his hair, leaving it in an adorable mess. My heart softened the smallest bit at his genuine distress. "I didn't know she was going to turn up here on the lake. Fuck." He kicked the trash can with his barefoot and winced. The contents scattered across the immaculate deck.

Fear gripped my insides. I had to ask the question. I had to know. "Do you—do you still love her?"

His sudden display of frustration released my pent up tears. I knew this happiness had been too good to be true. Weariness dragged over me. I bent to pick up my towel, hoping to hide my hurt from him, but a tiny sob slipped out before I could stop it. In two strides, he was at my side. Strong arms circled my shoulders, and tender hands smoothed up my back.

"No, no, no. Baby, no. Don't cry. I'm so sorry." The textured richness of his voice reverberated through his chest and into mine. His fingers dug into my hair as he pressed my face to his chest. "I never want to make you cry. Not ever."

Even though his words consoled me, I couldn't stop the sobs. I'd always been the strong one, the responsible one, the rock. Once the dam containing my self-control cracked, tears flooded down my cheeks. While I trembled, Tucker's hand cupped the nape of my neck. The tenderness of the gesture filled the empty spaces inside me and shored up my weakness. That's what he did for me. He was my white knight, always coming to my rescue.

"Damn, I'm a selfish bastard, aren't I? I didn't even think about how you'd feel." His fingers tangled in my hair while he murmured. "Maybe I loved her once. Not now. She doesn't matter to me. Not anymore." I rested my cheek against his chest and tried to pull it together. The scent of his shampoo mingled with the lake water in his damp hair. "You mean too much to me."

We stood on the deck, arms wrapped around each other, while I regained my composure. The wind picked up and rocked the boat beneath us. I swallowed and blinked swollen eyes. Tucker leaned back to see my face. He swiped a thumb over my cheeks to brush away the wetness.

"You should talk to her," I blurted. The notion pained me in ways I never imagined. Sydney still had some kind of hold over him, evident by the palpable connection between them, and that meant there were unresolved feelings on both sides. Until he got to the bottom of their breakup, I couldn't start a relationship with him, couldn't risk my heart.

"What?" His eyes narrowed.

I drew in a breath and tried again. "You need to sort out whatever it is—or was—between you. I don't think we can be together unless you know it's really over."

"I don't want to be with her." He opened his mouth to say more. I stopped him with a finger to his lips.

"And I can't be with you until I know she's out of the picture. As long as this—this—thing is unresolved, you're always going to wonder. And I'll always worry that I wasn't your first choice."

He pulled my hand away from his mouth. "Let's get something clear. I don't want her. I want you. Only you." The reflection of the water danced across his face, high-lighting the sculpted features. "If I wanted her, I wouldn't be here with you. I don't play those kinds of games."

"But she's—you know—*perfect*." The ferocity in his gaze frightened me a little. There was nothing playful about him now.

"She's not perfect. Maybe on the outside, but on the inside, she's selfish and vain and values fame over love." His voice softened to a sweet caress. "But you, little one, you're the most selfless person I've ever met. I think I fell in love with you the very first time I saw you with Hank." My heart rattled against my ribs. He loved me. *Me.* Fallon Young-blood. "The way you take care of him. You're kind and sweet and patient. You're the type of girl I want in my life." His eyes scanned my face, as if memorizing every line. "You make me believe in God and fairytales and happily-ever-after. Maybe even unicorns." He winked, and I couldn't help the smile stretching my cheeks.

"Oh." I blinked back tears of joy. No one had ever said anything like that to me before.

"If I made you feel any other way, then I must be doing

something wrong." He linked his fingers through mine and tugged me toward the cabin.

"Where are we going?"

"Down below." He stopped long enough to throw a mischievous grin over his shoulder. "Apparently, I need to teach you a lesson."

26

———

TUCKER

I sank into the sweet, wet heat of Fallon's pussy with a groan. She bucked her hips, twisting beneath me. I kept the pace slow, torturing her with long, deep thrusts. This was all about her, showing her how much she meant to me, loving her. Because I did love her. Seeing Sydney today proved it to me. I felt nothing for Syd but dislike and annoyance. Fallon, on the other hand, wrecked me in a dozen different ways. She hadn't said she loved me, but I knew she did. I saw it in the shine of her eyes and felt it in the tenderness of her touch. I had to be the luckiest bastard on the earth.

Soft gasps escaped her lips every time I pushed into her. If I had my way, by the time we were done, she'd have no doubts about my feelings. I peppered kisses along her throat, collarbone, and over the tops of her breasts. It took all my self-control to keep from pounding into her like some sex-starved animal. I rallied my control and pulled out all the way. A scowl furrowed her brow, and I smiled. That meant she liked it, wanted it, craved it like I did. She reached between us, to put me inside her again, but I grabbed her hand.

"What are you doing?" Her breasts rose and fell in short, rapid pants. Those pretty amber eyes widened. "Tucker!"

"Look at me." She stared back at me obediently. A small smile ghosted her mouth. I nudged my cock inside her, slowly, one deliberate inch at a time. Her eyes began to close. I stopped moving. "No. Right here. Eyes on mine." Our gazes locked once more. I loved her large, expressive eyes, the different shades of gold, liquid and watchful, like the eyes of a lioness. I pressed onward.

"Mmmm. Oh, Tucker." She drew in a shaky breath.

"Now tell me. Who loves you?" I withdrew and waited for her answer.

"You do?" The tip of her tongue slid across her lower lip. She was needy and wanton, the way I liked her.

"Good girl." I shoved in, hard and deep, all the way to the root. A delicious wave of ecstasy raced up my spine. Too long at this game, and I'd lose my shit. I was rewarded by the bite of her nails in my back.

"You're killing me, Tucker." She arched her back, tilting her hips, jerking impatiently.

"That so?" I sat back on my heels and stared down at her. Her long legs were bent at the knees, parted for me. Fine brown curls glistened between her thighs, wet from her arousal. The twin mounds of her small breasts jiggled, the nipples tight and pink. I sucked the tip of one into my mouth and let it go with a *pop*. "I don't think anyone ever died from sex."

"I need you. Inside me. Now." She twitched her bottom.

"Ask me nicely." I positioned my erection at the juncture of her thighs and nudged the tight walls of her entrance. She smiled and took my breath away.

"Please, Tucker?" When I didn't move, the playful tone of her voice turned forceful. "Oh, my God. Please, fuck me. Right now. I need to come. You're making me crazy."

"Well, that wasn't very nice." I eased into her, biting back a smile. "But okay." She groaned in relief and frustration. Her legs locked around my waist. I had her right where I wanted her. Or maybe she had *me* right where she wanted me. I wasn't sure who was in control any longer. Having the upper hand wasn't the most important aspect. It didn't really matter who drove the ship, as long as we sailed together.

I rode her like it was the first time, the last time, the only time we'd be together. She took me to a place I'd never been before, somewhere I never wanted to leave. If this was love, then hell yes, I was all in. The sadness, the anguish—they dissolved. That's what she did for me. She healed me in the way only a woman can—the right woman.

We went at it like rabbits, for hours, until we were both boneless and limp. Time lost all meaning. The boat swayed to a quiet rhythm. Smooth sheets felt cool against my sunburn, and the scent of lake water mingled with Fallon's shampoo. Daylight dimmed and filled the cabin with an orange glow. I had things to do, places to go. I needed to pack for my business trip, tidy up loose ends before I left, but none of it mattered. I watched her sleep, filled with a peace I'd never known.

27

FALLON

When it was time for the charity dinner, my heart thudded against the walls of my chest like a jackhammer. I hadn't seen Tucker all week, but we'd talked on the phone twice a day every day. His lazy drawl was the last thing I heard before bed and the first thing I heard in the morning. The old adage was true—absence made the heart grow fonder. I couldn't wait to see him again. Because his plane had been delayed, we agreed to meet at the country club. I was excited to see him and pressed nervous hands to the bodice of my dress.

I was also nervous for Hank. It was his first public outing since the accident. He looked smart in a rented tuxedo and bright blue bowtie. His eyes shone with excitement. Abe hovered at his left side, a giant in a somber black suit. Having him around eased a lot of my anxieties. His quiet capability gave Hank security and offered a male presence. Venetia met us at the doors to the ballroom, resplendent in a silver floor-length sheath. She hooked an arm through my elbow.

"We've got a table at the front. You're sitting with me

and Beckett. Sam and Dakota couldn't make it, but they sent their best," she said. "And Sam wrote a big fat check for the foundation." She carried an aura of vitality and command about her. "There are lots of important people here. Some of them are interested in starting the foundation for Hank. I'll introduce you later."

"Oh, okay." I suddenly felt very small and out of my element. I scanned the sea of people for Tucker's familiar face but only saw strangers. *You can do this, Fallon.* I squared my shoulders. I had this.

"If there's anything you need, let me know." She bent down to smile into my brother's eyes. "We're so honored to have you here, Hank. Thank you for coming."

An usher opened the double doors into the ballroom. I sucked in an awed breath. The expansive ceiling arched high over our heads, painted like a summer sky, held up by tall Grecian columns. The walls and floors gleamed of alabaster marble. Appointments of red and gold decorated the white tables. My insides began to quake. I'd never seen anything so grand.

"What do you think?" Venetia asked. The golden upsweep of her hair reflected the light from enormous crystal chandeliers.

"It's a little overwhelming," I said. "I didn't realize there would be so many people." My gaze followed men dressed in designer tuxedos, women wearing elaborate evenings gowns and dripping in jewels. I fingered the plain gold chain around my neck.

"Only two hundred and fifty of our closest friends at a thousand dollars a plate." She patted my arm. "Don't be nervous."

"Easy for you to say." I resisted the urge to roll my eyes. She laughed. I smiled back at her, feeling a bit of relief.

"They're just people, like you and me." She pointed to a couple at the nearest table. "That guy got so drunk at the last function he fell into the swimming pool. His wife is sleeping with her tennis instructor. I could go on, but you get the picture."

The tiny hairs on my arms prickled with awareness. I turned and found Tucker at my side. Hazel eyes and sensitive lips smiled back at me. The cadence of my heart increased. He leaned in for a kiss, his mouth brushing mine lightly. Before he pulled away, he whispered in my ear, "You look amazing."

"Thank you." My cheeks warmed as his gaze drifted down the length of my nude-colored gown, on loan from Venetia. Shimmering gold leaves peppered the skirt. The bodice hugged my small breasts, made higher by a torturous push-up bra. He fingered the delicate spaghetti strap crossing my shoulder before placing his hand on the small of my back.

"I can't wait to take this off you." The low timbre of his voice sent a thrill into my deepest recesses.

"Wait till you see what I'm wearing underneath," I said, thinking of the garter belt and stockings Venetia had insisted I purchase. His eyes darkened.

"And that's my cue to leave," Venetia said. She gave me a wink before turning toward a group of new guests.

After Tucker greeted Abe and Hank, he threaded his fingers through mine and pulled me to an alcove. Once we were safely hidden behind the damask drapes, he ran his nose along the length of mine and kissed the tip. I placed my hands on his broad chest and drew in a lungful of his clean, masculine scent. A simple black tuxedo hugged the width of his shoulders and narrow waist. He wore a plain black shirt beneath it, throat open, sans tie. We swayed into each other, savoring a rare moment alone.

With two steps, he backed me up against the wall and sealed his mouth over mine. I clutched the lapels of his jacket. His chest felt hard and solid against my breasts. Our tongues tangled together in a deep, wet kiss. I groaned into his mouth. I never wanted to let him go, to prolong the moment forever, to lose myself in everything Tucker. Outside the alcove, the band began to play jazz music. He sighed and pulled away.

"I missed you," he said.

"I missed you, too." I placed a kiss on the hollow of his throat. The collar of his shirt was open, exposing a small triangle of tanned skin, my current favorite body part. I pressed a kiss there, too, then lifted an eyebrow. "No tie? Isn't that part of the dress code?"

"Not for me." He smiled down into my eyes, setting off tiny explosions of heat beneath my skin. "I'm not really into the whole formalwear deal. I only wore this monkey suit so you wouldn't be embarrassed." Nothing could be farther from the truth. I saw the way other women looked at him, with equal parts admiration and lust. I smoothed a palm down the placket of his shirt. I still couldn't believe he was with me, that I was his girlfriend.

"You're so handsome, and I'm proud to be seen with you, no matter what you're wearing." I stood on tiptoe and trailed my fingertips over the clean shaven line of his jaw.

"You have to say that because you're my girlfriend." Mischief sparkled in his eyes.

"Maybe." I smiled back at him and brushed away the smudge of my lipstick on his lower lip.

"What do you mean? Maybe you have to say that? Or maybe you're my girlfriend?" He lifted a quizzical brow.

"Oh, I'm definitely your girlfriend." We beamed at each other. I savored the solidity of his body beneath my palms, the musk of his aftershave, and the heat in his eyes. How did I ever get so lucky?

"I guess we should get out there. People will start to talk." He looked at me wistfully. His hand drifted down to squeeze my bottom.

"Do we have to?" The idea of mingling with the cream of society's crop set my nerves on edge.

"Don't get all flighty. You look stunning, and you're with me. Just be yourself. People will love you." He waited while I smoothed my hair then hooked my hand through his elbow. "I know I do."

With Tucker at my side, we circulated the room, checking out the auction items, chatting with his acquaintances. He kept his hand on my waist. Although he strayed now and then, chatting to an acquaintance or business contact, his gaze remained on me. I'd never been particularly shy but found myself speechless in front of the governor, a Wimbledon tennis champion, and a Grand Prix race car driver. By the time we reached our table, the first course had been placed at our seats. My mind whirled with the names and faces of the people I'd met. Tucker held my hand beneath the table.

After the meal, Abe took an exhausted Hank back to the house, and the winning bids were announced for the silent auction. I listened in shock at the exorbitant price paid for a guitar autographed by rock star Elijah Crowe from the band Seven Drift. It was more than double my yearly salary.

"Did you bid on anything?" I asked Tucker.

"I did." The corners of his mouth curled upward like commas.

"Like what?"

"None of your business, that's what." He caressed one of my cheeks with the back of his finger. The promise in his gaze caused my breath to catch in my throat. "You'll just have to wait and see. I hope you like it."

"You guys are so cute." Venetia grinned across the table at us. My face heated.

"Yeah, you guys are *so* fucking cute." Beckett smirked then winced when Venetia pushed his shoulder. "You're making me look bad in front of my lady. I'm going to have to up my game to compete." He caught her hand in his, and the two shared a fiery but loving glare. She tried to pull away, but not before he dropped a tender kiss on her knuckles. Her frown softened into a flirtatious smile. I liked the easy playfulness of their relationship. They seemed so in love, so happy.

"Ignore them." Tucker nipped the tip of my finger lightly, stealing back my focus. I curled my hand around his, enjoying the friction of his palm against mine. He leaned forward and whispered in my ear, sending a frisson of excitement down my neck. "Let's get out of here."

Before I could reply, a commotion near the entrance broke my concentration. Two men dressed in black suits, wearing earpieces, broke apart to reveal Sydney. She wore a form-fitting red dress, slit high on the thigh, the neckline plunging almost to her navel. The moisture left my mouth followed by a sharp pang of jealousy. A hum of interest rippled around the room. Every male pair of eyes swiveled to admire her—every pair but Tucker's. His eyes narrowed, and his jaw tensed.

"What's she doing here?" The edge in his voice, sharp and angry, caused me to flinch.

"She overheard me talking about it and wanted to come. I couldn't say no." Venetia scowled at him. "She's a celebrity. She'll bring a lot of attention to the event."

Tucker sighed. "She better not cause any shit." Tension clipped his words. "I mean it, V."

"She promised to behave." Venetia's concerned glance caught mine. She worried her lower lip between her teeth. "Oh, dear. Are you going to be uncomfortable, Fallon? I didn't mean to cause a problem."

"No. It's fine." I drew in a deep breath and gave her a confident smile. Tucker's hand rested on my knee. I placed my hand on top of his and squeezed. The concern in his eyes told me everything I needed to know, shored up my insecurities, and left me glowing, breathless. "I'm good."

"You know I love you, right?" A dimple appeared beside his mouth. He leaned forward and pressed a kiss on my forehead.

"Yes, I know." I hadn't told him how I felt yet. The words swelled inside me. He needed to know how much I cared. Why had I waited so long? With Sydney's appearance, it seemed more important than ever to express my emotions, to let him know he meant everything to me.

"You love her? _Love_ her?" Beckett voice boomed across the table, closing my window of opportunity and turning heads at the table next to us. "Do my ears deceive me?" Tucker flushed a deep red. Venetia laughed, and I bit my lip to keep from joining her. "All I can say is...about fucking time."

"Beckett!" Venetia put a finger on his lips. "Hush, baby."

"Sorry." He wrapped a long arm around her waist and

pulled her into his lap. She squirmed in protest. "Get over here, woman. Damn, you make me hot when you're bossy like that."

"Seriously, Beckett. Not here." She wiggled in her fiancé's arms. He tightened his grip and nuzzled her earlobe.

"We need to go. I'll have the car brought around front." Tucker stood and pulled me to my feet alongside him. "Let's say our goodbyes."

"Okay. I'm going to visit the powder room first. Meet you at the doors?" Anticipation continued building inside me. Tucker's gaze lingered on my mouth a fraction longer than appropriate. I wasn't sure what he had in mind for the rest of the evening, but I couldn't wait to find out.

28

TUCKER

I watched Fallon disappear toward the restroom while I waited for the valet to bring my car around. The silk of her dress hugged her backside. The hem swirled around her ankles as she walked. I couldn't wait to get my hands on her round, sweet bottom, and peel away the layers of her clothing to reveal all her pink parts. It would be our first night alone. Abe had agreed to stay with Hank until morning. Hillary and Les would be there for backup, if he required help. I whistled a happy tune and leaned against the wall, hands in my pockets.

"Tucker."

I knew that voice. My euphoria shriveled up and died. Sydney moved into my line of sight. Her pouty mouth curved into a smile, resplendent with white teeth and red lipstick. She touched my arm. I pulled it out of her reach and didn't smile back.

"I was hoping you'd be here." Her blue eyes searched my face. "You don't look happy to see me."

I didn't reply. Instead, I angled my torso away from her and prayed the valet would hurry. A society event was hardly the place to air out grievances. I couldn't guarantee my temper would remain in check, and I didn't want to ruin Venetia's event or embarrass Fallon.

"Really?" She arched a winged eyebrow. "You're going to stand there and ignore me?"

"I've got nothing to say to you, Syd." I shoved my hands deeper into my pockets and clenched them into fists.

"Give me two minutes." Her china doll features sobered. "Please? And I swear I'll never bother you again."

I rested my head against the wall behind me and studied the ornate scrollwork of the ceiling overhead. Sydney had the tenacity of a bulldog. I knew she wouldn't give up until I gave her a chance to say whatever it was she had pent up inside her. And some small part of me needed closure. "Fine. Two minutes. Not one second longer."

She flashed her blinding smile, complete with dimples, took my arm, and dragged me onto the balcony overlooking the lake. Torches lit the iron railing. Their flames danced in the summer breeze and cast golden reflections on the water below. Stars winked in an inky black sky where the moon shone like a polished pearl.

"How have you been? You look great." She dragged her gaze up and down the length of me, eyes heavy-lidded and thick with bristly lashes. Once upon a time, that look had sent my cock into full alert. Tonight, I only felt annoyed. I scrubbed a hand over my face, certain this was a bad idea.

"I'm not interested in small talk. Say what you've got to say. Fallon's going to be waiting for me." I heaved a sigh, wearied by her presence, eager to get back to my girl. *My girl.* The one I loved. The one who mattered.

"She seems nice." She studied my face, searching for a way past my defenses. I squared my shoulders. "I was surprised to hear you were together."

"I don't know why. Fallon's the best thing that ever happened to me," I said, daring her to say one wayward thing about Fallon.

"Oh." Her face fell a little. I didn't want to hurt her, but she needed to understand my position. "I'm sure she is." She drew in a deep breath. "So, you guys are serious?"

"Very." I stared at her. She blinked and looked down at her feet, encased in complicated, strappy sandals. I glanced at my watch. "Is that it?" I moved toward the door.

"No. Wait. Please." Her voice softened. She grabbed my arm, and I flinched. Her next words tumbled out in a rush. "What I did was wrong, and I'm so sorry. I hurt you. I didn't realize how much I loved you, how painful it would be to see you with someone else. I screwed up, Tucker. I know that now. I came back here to ask for a second chance. To tell you I made a mistake. You have to forgive me. You have to." Tears flooded her cheeks, smudging her mascara.

"You didn't hurt me, Sydney. You *crushed* me." I stared back at her, unaffected by the waterworks. She'd played me one time too many. I had no idea if she was acting now or genuine. I didn't really care. I only remembered the months of anguish, the sleepless nights, the endless need to taunt death in the aftermath of her betrayal. "That's not how you treat someone you love."

"I know. I know. I was all messed up in my head. My agent kept telling me I had to marry Alex, that it was good for my career, and the studio wouldn't let me out of my contract. I've been so miserable. You have no idea what I've been through. Alex has a girlfriend. He's been cheating on me since before the wedding." She swiped at her tears with the back of her hand. "He drinks all the time, and he never comes home at night. I filed for divorce last month."

"I'm sorry you're so unhappy." I shook my head and put a hand on the door, my patience gone.

"You're leaving?" Her eyebrows lifted in incredulity. "Did you hear what I said? I love you. I came back to be with you." She threw her arms around my neck. "Tucker? Please tell me it's not too late."

With the gentlest touch I could muster, I disentangled her arms and held them at her sides. "You should've been honest with me from the start, Syd. You lied to me. You led me on. You married someone else. Why, in God's name, would I want to be with someone who treated me like that?"

She trembled from head to toe. "I can make it up to you. I'll do anything. Don't make me beg, Tucker, because I will."

She'd fucked up in a major way, destroying our friendship and any love I might have felt for her, but I couldn't be mean to her. I'd loved her once, even if it had been misguided. "There's nothing you can do. I love Fallon. With all my heart." The strength of my feelings overshadowed any anger or animosity for Sydney's actions. My broken heart had led me to a new and better love, and I had Sydney to thank for that. "I wish you all the best."

"But what am I going to do?" She stared at me, her face pale, eyes swollen and red-rimmed.

"I don't know." I opened the door and gave her one last look over my shoulder. "You should've thought of that before you fucked me over."

29

FALLON

Tucker's face lit up when he saw me walking down the hallway. He leaned one shoulder against the wall, feet crossed at the ankles, hands in his pockets. He straightened as I approached. My body responded to the fire in his gaze, nipples tightening, my blood heating. He was too beautiful, too perfect to be real, and he was mine. Streaks of gold brightened his dark blond hair and sparked in the stubble shadowing his jaw. His nostrils flared as I approached, a primal reaction that arrowed straight between the legs. I felt a ridiculous ping inside my chest, like a champagne bubble about to burst.

"Are you ready?" When I drew close enough, he dropped a kiss on the top of my head.

"Sure." I beamed back at him, loving the way his fingers tangled with mine, the longing in his eyes, and the flutter of anticipation in my belly.

"Mr. Spaulding? I'm so glad I caught you." We turned in unison to find one of the auction stewards rushing toward us. He flashed an apologetic smile in my direction. "I apologize for the intrusion."

"Can I help you?" Tucker asked. He tugged at the cuffs of his shirt. In his jeans and T-shirt, it was easy to peg him as a bohemian playboy. With his tailored suit and impossibly square jaw, he looked every inch the businessman. He'd done well for himself, and I couldn't be prouder to be at his side.

"Sir, you've won the bid for one of the auction items. Could I get you to sign before you go? It will speed up the sale process. If you don't mind, that is."

"Is it okay?" Tucker asked me. "I'll just be a second."

"Sure. It's fine. I'll wait here for you," I said. He lifted my hand to his lips and kissed my fingertips. "What did you get?"

"A trip for two to Tahiti." He bit his lower lip and waggled his eyebrows. "For you and me. Two weeks of nothing but sun, sand, and surf."

The idea of a vacation in paradise with Tucker made my head spin. I clasped my hands together to keep from jumping up and down like a little kid. "Really? Are you serious?"

"You know it. Back in a flash, baby cakes." He winked and followed the steward into one of the offices at the end of the hall.

After a few minutes, I grew bored and wandered the hallway. Original framed artwork lined the walls of the corridor. I was too excited to stand still, eager for my first night with Tucker and my first night away from Hank since his accident. A sense of giddy euphoria buoyed my steps. It felt good to be normal, to act my age, to be free from worry for the space of an evening.

Through a set of glass double doors, I spied the shimmering waters of the lake. I needed a breath of fresh air to cool my heated cheeks and clear my head. I pressed through the doors and out onto the balcony. The songs of crickets and frogs filled the night. The scent of roses carried on the air. I paused at the railing to take in the serenity of the water.

Tonight, I planned to tell Tucker how much he meant to me. I was ashamed for waiting so long, when I'd known for months. My cheeks heated at the thought of sleeping in his bed, waking up in his arms. A tumble of butterflies erupted in my tummy. It had been a long time since I'd spent the night with a guy, and never with one I loved.

"Fallon? Hi." A tentative voice jerked me from reverie.

"Ah!" I dropped my clutch on the balcony floor and jumped backward. At the sight of Sydney's face floating in the darkness, I placed a hand over my heart and gasped. "You scared the crap out of me."

"I'm sorry," she said. "I didn't mean to startle you." In the flickering torchlight, I saw the smudges of mascara on her cheeks and her puffy eyes. She looked broken, defeated.

"Are you okay?" I didn't care for her, but I hated to see anyone in distress.

"Yes. No." A hiccup shook her shoulders. Her self-control seemed ready to snap in two. "No, I'm not." She pillowed her face in her hands and sobbed.

I watched helplessly, uncertain if I should offer her comfort. I understood how it felt to be devastated, to make mistakes, to lose someone you loved. The circumstances of our losses differed, but her pain seemed just as real. After an uncomfortable minute, she collected herself and drew in a deep, shuddering breath.

"He doesn't love me anymore." She sank onto the stone bench between us and looked up at me with round, sad eyes. "I ruined everything between us."

"Oh." I shifted from one foot to the other and glanced at the doors, wishing Tucker would hurry the hell up.

"Do you love him?" She searched my face. "I mean, really love him?"

"I do." I nodded and tried to swallow down the thickness in my throat. In spite of my jealousy, I still felt compassion for her. She'd had a wonderful guy and had thrown him away, something she'd regret for the rest of her life.

She twisted her hands in her lap. "He loves you, too. He told me so. Tucker's not the kind of guy to say something like that if he didn't mean it." A wry smile ghosted her mouth. "I'd really like to hate you, but I can't. Venetia says you're awesome. Even Beckett likes you. Just the fact that you're standing here with me proves you're a nice person."

"Um, thank you?" I shifted toward the exit.

"I should get back out there. Circulate." She drew out a tiny compact to observe the damage to her cosmetics. "I'm a mess."

"You're lovely," I said, sincerely. Even with tearstained cheeks, her beauty surpassed anyone I'd ever met. "I'm sure there's a guy out there dying for a chance to go out with you."

"Really?" Her persona brightened, and a bit of the sparkle returned to her eyes. "You're very sweet." She drew in a deep breath and stood, smoothing her dress over her hips. The transformation unfolded right before me. She went from sobbing mess to movie star in the blink of an eye. "The paparazzi are vultures, you know. If they get a whiff of a story, my face will be all over the tabloids tomorrow." Her lips curved to reveal perfect white teeth in a sassy smile. "I can do this, right?"

"I think you can." I smiled back at her, more than a little impressed with her strength.

"Before you go, could you do me a favor?" With a tube of lipstick, she swiped color over her lips, pressing them together before she continued. "Take care of him, would you? He's one in a million."

30

———

FALLON

From the edge of Tucker's king-size bed, I waited for him to join me. His house bordered the lake, a three-story modern monstrosity of glass and steel. A wall of windows faced me, providing an unobstructed view of the water and the full moon. I removed my shoes and aligned them neatly beside the bed. The sounds of him moving around the house, locking doors, closing windows, echoed up the stairs. Sweat dampened my palms. I was in his house, his bedroom, his *bed*. We were spending the night together, as a couple. Anxiety knotted in my chest. This was so much more than I'd ever imagined for myself, for us.

To calm my nerves, I wandered the expanse of his bedroom, which occupied the entire third floor. A living space, enormous flat-screen TV, and fireplace took up one-third of the far end. I trailed my fingertips over the buttery black leather of the sofa. Personal items were scattered here and there; a worn pair of hiking boots, a rumpled sweatshirt, the hoodie he'd worn on the elevator before my interview at Twisted Wire Productions. I picked it up, rubbing the fabric between my fingers. I sniffed; it smelled like him, a mixture of peppermint and his shower gel. The connecting door at my left led into an enormous bathroom, complete with walk-in shower and a bathtub the size of a small swimming pool. The minimalist furnishings echoed Tuck's penchant for modern conveniences down to the intricate panel of buttons and switches next to the doors.

The iron bed floated in the center of the room, anchored by an even larger black wool rug. I curled my toes in the long fibers before climbing into the middle of the mattress. Should I take off my dress? Or would that be too slutty? After a second of contemplation, I wiggled out of it and slid between the cool zillion thread count sheets, wearing nothing but the pushup bra, skimpy lace panties, stockings and garter belt. A naughty thrill chased away my nerves. I couldn't wait to be in his arms again, loving him, being loved by him.

I heard his footsteps echo down the hall, drawing closer. My pulse accelerated. I wanted this to be as special for him as it was for me. In a fit of indecision, I turned off the lamp beside the bed then turned it on again. This was so totally unlike me; I had no idea how to be sexy or seductive. The door handle clicked and a frisson of fear and anticipation hit me straight in my most intimate parts. The waiting was killing me.

Tucker came through the door and stopped dead at the sight of me in his bed. "Wow," he said, in a throaty whisper. He came to the edge of the mattress and stared down at me, his eyes filled with dark, liquid heat. "Are you ready for me?"

"Yes." Oh God, yes. I was *so* ready for him. Just seeing him there, wanting me, his arousal visible in the flare of his nostrils and the bulge inside his pants—it was all the fore-play I needed. I rubbed my thighs together, feeling the dampness inside my panties. He licked his lips and an arrow of need stabbed my womb.

"You have no idea how much I've missed you," he said, his voice a ragged mixture of emotion and lust. "I can't wait to get inside you."

"Then get inside me." I lifted to my knees and clutched the sheet at my chest. I grabbed the waistband of his trousers and tugged him closer. "What are you waiting for?"

"Don't rush me." A playful smile tugged the corners of his mouth. "I want to enjoy this. I want to savor you."

No words had ever affected me more or inspired a greater thrill. With agonizing slowness, he unbuttoned his shirt then tossed it aside. I bit my lower lip. The sight of his lean body, the grooves of muscle on his hips, the swell of his pectorals—they undid my self-control. I wanted him, needed him, had to have him. My nipples tightened to painful points. I threw aside the sheet and lay in front of him, wanton and ready.

He climbed onto the bed and walked up the mattress on his knees. I opened my legs so he could settle inside the V of my thighs. "What have we here?" he asked. As he spoke, he curled a finger inside one of my garters, pulled it away from my skin, then released it with a snap. A surprised giggle popped out of my mouth. He dragged his gaze down the length of my body and back to my eyes. "You take my breath away, Fallon. I hope you know what you do to me."

"No. I don't. Tell me. What do I do to you?" I walked my fingers down the hills and valleys of his abs to cup the erection between his legs, thick behind his zipper. "Is this what I do to you?"

"Yes." He groaned and pressed into my palm. "I'm going to eat you up, baby girl." The way he was looking at me, a combination of playfulness and heat, suggested he was going to devour me. "All of you. From the tips of your toes to the end of your nose." He bit the body part in question. I shuddered, my body alight with electricity. "You're not going to need these." With a rip and a snap, he twisted the fragile side elastic of my panties. The sheer lace whispered over my pussy as he dropped them onto the floor.

"Tucker, those were brand new." I pretended to pout.

"What? I'll buy you more." He trailed a hot line of hot kisses along my throat, my collarbone, ending up between my breasts. "I'll buy you anything you want. Anything, Fallon. Name it and it's yours."

"What I want can't be bought with money." Things were getting serious. The ache between my legs intensified. He sucked a nipple into his mouth, swirled his tongue around the tip then blew cool air onto it. I tried to squirm away from the overload of pleasure, but he pressed me into the mattress with a hand on my belly. I moaned. "You don't play fair."

"Tell me." He paused to lock eyes with me. "What do you want from me?" He continued his descent down my ribs, the slope of my tummy, and kissed each of my pelvic bones.

What was he doing to me? I was going to come undone, lose my shit, right in front of him. I'd never been so totally lost in a guy before, but it was too late. I'd already given him my heart and my soul. Now he wanted my body, and I was going to hand it over without a second thought.

"I want you, Tucker." My voice sounded unrecognizable, harsh from the rapid panting of my breaths. He dipped his tongue into the slit between my legs. The combination of wet and heat shocked my system. I moaned and twisted, trying to get away and draw closer at the same time.

"I'm already yours. Name something else." The pressure of his tongue increased. He eased one finger inside me, then two, slipping and sliding through my wetness.

"I want to be happy, safe, secure." It was all I'd ever wanted, really. "I want Hank to be happy, too."

He sat up to stare at me, but kept his fingers inside me, stroking and teasing. "You're safe with me. Always. I promise, baby."

I arched as he wrung every drop of orgasm out of me. When I was finished, my breasts heaving, lungs aching, I lay in a sweating mess beneath him. My limbs felt weak and boneless, my eyelids heavy, drugged. He shifted his weight onto his elbows. His erection bobbed between us, thick and hard, nudging my thigh.

"Don't you fall asleep on me." His amused chuckle roused me from a haze of sexual fog. "I'm not done with you. Not even close."

"I love you." The admission rolled off my tongue. The emotion burned inside my chest, too enormous to be contained any longer.

"I know." He smacked my thigh.

"Ouch! What was that for?" My eyes snapped open. He grinned down at me, a devilish light in his eyes.

"For waiting so long to tell me."

FALLON

I awoke to an amazing view of the sunrise outside Tucker's bedroom. Streaks of orange and pink lit the water on fire. I paused long enough to admire the scene then slid from the bed. I tiptoed around the room in search of my clothing. Tucker stirred and gave me a lazy smile.

"I'm sorry," I said. "I didn't mean to wake you." Our gazes connected with the kind of intimacy that comes from sharing secrets and truths. The space between my legs throbbed and ached where he'd ridden me over and over throughout the night. We'd managed to squeeze in a few hours of sleep. I was exhausted in the best kind of way.

"What are you doing?" He propped his head up with an elbow and watched as I got down on hands and knees to search beneath the bed for my bra.

"I need to get home. Hank will be up soon." I found my garter belt and shoved it into the overnight bag I'd brought along, filled with a few basic toiletries and a change of clothes.

"What time does he wake up?"

"Around eight." My stockings were piled in a knot on the end of the bed. I tossed them into the bag as well.

"It's six o'clock. You live two miles away. There's plenty of time." His lips curved in amusement.

"Well, I'll need to take a shower. He won't know what to think if I'm not there." I turned in a circle, scanning the room for more articles of lingerie. "I need to be there."

"No, you don't. Abe is there. Hillary and Les, too." He patted the bed beside him. "Come back to bed so I can love you some more."

I hesitated, drawn to the promise in his eyes and the warmth of his body. "No, I can't. I've always been there in the morning." I made certain to greet him each day. My presence provided stability for him. "He won't know what to think if I'm not there."

"He knows you're with me. We talked it over. He's good with it." Tucker crooked a finger. "Now. You. In my bed. That's an order."

Being an obstinate creature, I stuck my tongue out at him. "You talked it over?" Tucker nodded. "When?"

"We had a video chat last week." He sat up and ran a hand though his hair. The ends stuck out in a sexy mess. Blond stubble covered his cheeks. His total hotness over-whelmed my weak defenses.

"Is that so?" My laughter felt good, like champagne bubbles on my tongue. "And how did you do that?"

"Abe's phone. Of course, I did all the talking." He snaked an arm around my waist and toppled me into the bed. "But I discovered this computer program that recog-nizes eye movements. He'll be able to type out messages, surf the net, stuff like that." As he talked, his knee wiggled between mine. I parted my thighs willingly. "I ordered one yesterday. We were going to surprise you with it on your birthday. Don't tell him I told you."

"What?" I jerked excitedly. Tears burned my eyes. The thought of holding a real conversation with Hank shook my world. "Are you kidding me?"

"Of course not." The focus of his concentration centered on adjusting my hips to align with his. He sank inside me, my channel slippery and tight. We groaned in unison. The delicious hardness of his cock heated my core.

We fell silent. The room filled with the sounds of flesh slapping against flesh, moans and sighs, the rustle of sheets. We dissolved into a writhing mass of clutching fingers, tangled limbs, and wandering lips. He used me, held me, caressed me like I was some fragile thing, precious and rare. In return, I gave everything I had back to him.

32

TUCKER

We finally rolled out of bed a little past noon. If I'd had my way, we would never have left, but I understood Fallon's concerns. Hank was more than a brother to her; he was her family, her life. I wanted to be the center of her world, but I was happy to share her attentions with someone as sweet as Hank. And I understood that they were a package deal, which was fine by me.

After a long and sexually fulfilling shower together, we headed downstairs into the kitchen. A handful of people milled about the room. Tyler and Tate sat at the breakfast bar, eating ice cream out of the carton with mixing spoons. Two of their friends lounged at the kitchen table, eyes glued to their phones. Tabitha, my only sister and Tyler's twin, sat on the kitchen counter, her bare feet swinging through the air.

Fallon stopped short at the entrance to the kitchen. She shrank behind me, her shyness adorable. I put an arm around her waist and tugged her forward.

"You didn't tell me there were people here," she whispered. I liked the way she burrowed into the nook of my shoulder, seeking my protection. "We were noisy."

"Don't worry. They didn't hear you screaming my name." I waggled my eyebrows. "At least not last night. They didn't get here until this morning. After that, I'm not so sure." She blushed to the roots of her hair.

"Dude, where are the keys to the jet skis?" Caleb came in the sliding patio doors, Roni on his heels.

"Here." I opened a drawer, drew out the keys and tossed them to him. He snatched them out of the air with one hand. "Make sure you fill up the gas tanks."

"Got it." Caleb's gaze met mine, and a knowing smirk curled his lips. "Hey, Fallon."

"Hi." She lifted her hand in a quiet wave. I paused to brush the hair back from her forehead and gave her a soft peck on the lips.

"Can I come with you?" Tabitha jumped off the counter, her feet smacking on the tile floor with the impact. She tossed her long blond hair over her shoulder and turned pleading eyes to Caleb.

Caleb stiffened, his gaze begging me for help. He leaned into my shoulder. "Man, your sister. Seriously. She will not get off my jock. She grabbed my ass." His eyebrows lifted in horror. "Twice."

"Can't help you there." I gave him a mock shove. "She's a kid. Be nice to her."

He groaned. Tabitha's enthusiasm for Caleb was legendary. "Fine. You can come. But you're riding with Roni. And don't touch me." He pointed a finger at her. "I mean it."

"What?" Tabby's face was the picture of innocence. She lifted her palms in the air. They left through the sliding doors, their banter trailing in their wake as they headed to the boathouse. The boys and their friends tumbled after them, trading playful punches, like a group of unruly puppies.

"Do you always have so many people here?" Fallon asked when they'd gone.

"Pretty much. The boys are here for the summer. Tabby's just visiting for the week. Caleb and Roni hang out on the weekends." I couldn't imagine an empty house, living alone. I'd grown accustomed to a houseful of friends and family. "I suppose it seems strange to you."

She tucked a wayward strand of hair behind her ear. "Yeah. It is, but I could get used to it, I think." Her amber eyes lifted to meet mine; soft, warm, heated. My gaze dipped to her lips. They were still red and swollen from my kisses.

"Come on. I want to show you the house." I threaded my fingers through hers, enjoying her smile. I pulled her from room to room, my chest filling with pride at the world I'd built for myself. I had more than enough money to last a lifetime. It all seemed pointless without someone to share in my prosperity.

"This is amazing, Tucker," she said at the end of the tour. She stood on the bottom step of the main staircase, putting her at my height. "You're amazing." My heart skipped a beat as she leaned forward to brush her lips over mine. "I'm so proud of you."

"Someday, I want to share this with you," I said. "I know it's too soon to talk about moving in together, but I think you should consider it." A dent formed between her brows, and I knew she was thinking about Hank. "Oh, no. Don't get all stubborn on me. Just hear me out. We can put an elevator here, build a wheelchair ramp outside. Or we can convert one of the rooms on the main floor for Hank. I've got eight bedrooms and a guesthouse for Hillary." I swiped away the tear on her cheek with the back of my index finger. "You've spent your entire adult life providing for someone else. I'm willing to share that responsibility with you. It's time to give someone else a shot. Let me keep you safe—both of you."

33

FALLON

On the drive back to my house, the world seemed to be a better place. Colors were brighter, the sun hotter, the sky bluer. I floated on a cloud of euphoria, my feet barely touching the ground. Tucker parked his black Maserati in the driveway behind Hillary's Honda. A flock of teenaged boys from the house across the street swarmed the car as Tucker opened my car door and helped me exit. I admired his patience, the quiet calm of his voice, the way he greeted them with a smile.

"Those kids are my bread and butter," he said, once the fray had dissipated. "Without them, I'd still be living in my parent's basement, or working in some boring nine-to-five job."

I lifted on tiptoe to plant a kiss on his cheek. "Your generosity is what makes me love you so much."

He put a hand on the small of my back and ushered me up the sidewalk. It seemed like I had left for the charity auction a lifetime ago. Everything seemed different but the same, new but unchanged.

Hillary met us at the door. Her eyes glimmered with tears. My heart skidded to a stop. Something was wrong. I knew it was too good to be true. No one could be this happy. Guilt rolled over me like a rogue wave. I should've been here for Hank. Spending the night with Tucker had been selfish, putting my needs ahead of Hank's welfare. I grabbed her arm.

"What? What is it?" Fear shook my voice. Tucker's arm tightened around my waist, shoring me up. I leaned into him, needing his strength. "Where's Hank?"

Hillary lifted a finger to her lips, gesturing for quiet. "He's fine. Come see," she said in a hushed whisper. She nodded toward the living room.

I peeked around the foyer wall, Tucker on my heels. Neve sat on the side of Hank's bed. Her right hand cupped his face. She leaned close, talking to him in a voice too low for me to hear. Tears streamed down her pretty face, glimmering in the sunlight streaming through the picture window. She stroked his temple, pushed the hair back from his forehead, and smiled into his eyes. Hank's lips curved in a smile. He looked young and happy. I blinked away tears of joy.

Tucker squeezed me tighter and pressed his lips against my ear. "Come on. Let's give them some privacy."

We went out to the front porch and sat on the swing. This was where we started, where it all began for us. Tucker held my hand as we rocked in the sunshine. Kids played soccer in the street. Laughter and music hovered in the air of the neighborhood. I marveled at the way my life had changed in the flutter of a hummingbird's wings. Four months ago, I'd been alone and on the verge of a breakdown. Now, I had a family and the love of a good man. Hank had a future. And I had the greatest gift of all. I had hope.

Thank you for reading Foolish Regrets. Be sure to check out the next book in the Seaforth Billionaires Series, Foolish Promises.

A marriage dragged through hell teeters on the brink of collapse by circumstances beyond their control.

Samuel Seaforth has enough money to last a lifetime, but there are things no amount of cash can buy. The one thing his wife wants is the one thing he can't give her. As they grow further apart, his feelings of helplessness grow stronger. And there's nothing he despises more than losing control.

When they remarried, Dakota thought she'd found her happily-ever-after. Instead, she found heartache like she'd never imagined possible. In order to stop the pain, she shuts down her emotions and exiles Sam from her heart.

Sam and Dakota are back for the next chapter in their love story. They've been married, divorced, and remarried. Their shared tragedy tears them apart in unexpected ways and brings them both to ask: if they had the chance to do it over again, would they?

If you loved the heat of Fifty Shades and the angst of the Crossfire Series, you'll want to one-click this billionaire romance today.

GET IT HERE >>> Foolish Promises

THE EXILED PRINCE WORLD
(In reading order)

The Exiled Prince

The Dirty Princess

The War King

The Royal Arrangement

The Rebel Queen

The Ruthless Knight

Absolute Power

Absolute Trust

SEAFORTH BILLIONAIRES SERIES

Foolish Mistakes

Foolish Deception

Foolish Secrets

Foolish Regrets

Foolish Promises

Foolish Dreams

Foolish Hearts

Foolish Lovers

Foolish Tears

Dirty Work

FELONY ROMANCE SERIES

Intoxicated

Unexpected

Vindicated

Impulsive

Drift

Committed

BAD BEHAVIOR SERIES

Bad Behavior #1

Bad Behavior #2

Bad Behavior #3

STANDALONES

Lies We Tell

SHORT STORIES

Everything

Linger

ABOUT THE AUTHOR

Jeana is a *USA Today* and *Publishers Weekly* bestselling author from Indiana. She gave up a career in the corporate world to write about sexy billionaires and alpha bad boys. With over twenty books, three series, and many awards beneath her belt, she's never regretted her choice to live out her dream. She's a free spirit, a wanderer at heart, and loves animals with a passion. When she's not tripping over random objects, you'll find her walking in the sunshine with her rambunctious dogs and dreaming about true love. Subscribe to Jeana's newsletter and get the inside scoop on new and upcoming releases, giveaways, and much more! SUBSCRIBE

9 781943 938896